Praise for Heather MacAllister...

"Witty, romantic, sexy and fun...
and Heather's books aren't bad, either."
—*New York Times* bestselling author
Christina Dodd

"Curling up with a Heather MacAllister romance is
one of my favorite indulgences."
—*New York Times* bestselling author
Debbie Macomber

"For quirky fun and sexy wit, Heather MacAllister
is my go-to author."
—Award-winning author Amanda Stevens

"Clever, funny and with a completely satisfying
ending, this is a must read."
—*RT Book Reviews* on *His Little Black Book*

"Great humor and great sex abound."
—*RT Book Reviews* on *Undressed*

"A one-sitting read for me. I got so caught up in
this story that I really didn't want it to end."
—*The Best Reviews* on *Male Call*

"The plot was inspired, the dialogue was witty and
the secondary characters were extraordinary."
—*Writers Unlimited* on
How to be the Perfect Girlfriend

Blaze

Dear Reader,

I've always been fascinated by the twelve days of extravagant Christmas gifts given by someone's true love in the carol. What was with all the poultry? Every year, there are articles about updating the gifts, but what I admire is the time and thought involved in giving presents for twelve days. You've really got to like somebody to go to that much trouble. I reversed things in *A Man for All Seasons* because Tyler discovers his childhood friend, Marlie, is his true love—but only *after* he gives her dates with twelve other men.

I hope you enjoy their story and Marlie's dates based on the "Twelve Days of Christmas."

Merry Christmas!

Heather MacAllister
www.HeatherMacAllister.com

Heather MacAllister

A MAN FOR ALL SEASONS

HARLEQUIN®

TORONTO • NEW YORK • LONDON
AMSTERDAM • PARIS • SYDNEY • HAMBURG
STOCKHOLM • ATHENS • TOKYO • MILAN • MADRID
PRAGUE • WARSAW • BUDAPEST • AUCKLAND

Recycling programs
for this product may
not exist in your area.

ISBN-13: 978-0-373-79587-1

A MAN FOR ALL SEASONS

Printed in U.S.A.

ABOUT THE AUTHOR

Heather MacAllister lives near the Texas gulf coast where, in spite of the ten-month growing season and plenty of humidity, she can't grow plants. She's a former music teacher who married her high school sweetheart on the 4th of July—is it any surprise that their two sons turned out to be a couple of firecrackers? Heather has written more than forty romantic comedies, which have been translated into twenty-six languages and published in dozens of countries. She's won a Romance Writers of America Golden Heart Award, *RT Book Reviews* awards for best Harlequin Romance and best Harlequin Temptation, and is a three-time RITA® Award finalist. When she's not writing stories where life has its quirks, Heather collects vintage costume jewelry, loves fireworks displays, computers that behave and sons who answer their mother's emails. You can visit her at www.HeatherMacAllister.com.

Books by Heather MacAllister

HARLEQUIN BLAZE
473—UNDRESSED
527—HIS LITTLE BLACK BOOK

To Andy,
my man for all seasons

1

"SORRY, SORRY, SORRY!" Marlie Waters winced at her house-mate's grim expression.

Tyler stood in the doorway of her home office and jammed his arms into his shirt sleeves. He looked exactly like a man who'd been about to get laid and had been interrupted. Because he had been. By her. Not the laying, the interrupting.

"I was distracted." Marlie gestured to her computer. "I was concentrating on the website and checking to make sure it looked the same in every browser and decided a snack sounded good and while I was thinking about code and something to eat, I wasn't thinking about you and…" *Your chest.*

Her gaze danced ahead of his fingers as he did up his shirt.

"Axelle." Tyler finished buttoning his shirt and glared at her, fists on his hips, his hair rumpled. A little smear of eye shadow gleamed on his cheek.

No doubt whatsoever about what he'd been doing on the big, brown, comfy sofa—and with whom—even though Marlie had raced back downstairs, eyes averted.

Awkward, yes, but more disconcerting was seeing her housemate as a desirable man through Axelle's slate-shadowed eyes instead of her own naked, puffy, over-worked ones.

Intellectually, Marlie had known Tyler was a good-looking guy, the All-American, touch-football-on-the-weekends type, but emotionally, he'd never pushed her buttons. She'd disconnected those buttons, anyway. Maybe forever. Life was much less stressful without those buttons connected.

But now, here he stood in all his rumpled, sexy glory, and right in the middle of her apologetic explanation, her buttons decided to reconnect themselves just in time for Tyler to lean on them.

Lust sucker-punched her.

Marlie needed a moment. Ty was like a brother—okay, never a brother. More like a cousin. Her gaze skipped over his face, gritted jaw, and the rise and fall of his chest. A really distant cousin. By marriage.

A muscle worked in the cheek unadorned by Axelle's eye shadow.

Tyler Burton, the son of longtime friends of her parents, her reluctant playmate on several joint family summer vacations, the sulking teen from their last, shared camping trip—*that* Tyler Burton—had grown into a manly man. One might say he was a hunk. Tyler inhaled deeply, his chest rising impressively before he exhaled in a whoosh. And that person would be Marlie.

How convenient that he was temporarily living with her and how incredibly remiss of her not to have taken advantage of that fact sometime in the past eighteen months.

Whoa. Marlie beat the lust back into long-term storage and summoned the memory of the skinny, surly Ty of her youth. "Axelle," she repeated to ground herself. Axelle, Ty's current girlfriend. And her client. In fact, Axelle's website was the one Marlie'd been working on this evening. She didn't think they'd appreciate the irony. "Anyway, I forgot you and Axelle were here when I came upstairs, and then I remembered and—"

"Screamed."

"It was more of a yelp."

The muscle twitched again.

"I'm sorry! I closed my eyes, I swear." Unfortunately not before the image of a shirtless Ty and, oh, this was not good, her shirtless client, was burned into her retinas.

"You spoiled the mood." Tyler tucked in his shirt and buckled his belt.

Marlie thought he'd been overdressed for a casual dinner at home, but Axelle's idea of casual was more upscale than hers. Probably a French thing. "You can get it back. I'll stay in my office for the rest of the night, I promise. Look, I'm shutting the door."

There was a rustling at the top of the stairs and Tyler glanced up before fixing Marlie with a look that told her their discussion wasn't over. "I'm driving Axelle home now."

Marlie went into her office and stayed there, anyway, but she could hear their voices murmuring. She couldn't make out what they were saying, so she pressed her ear against the door.

"But she never goes anywhere!" she heard a frustrated Ty protest.

"No boyfriend?" Axelle asked. "Well, no, she wouldn't I suppose." And the door to the garage closed.

Ouch. Ouch not because Marlie was pining for a boyfriend—she wasn't—but because in the nearly three years since Marlie *had* had a boyfriend—a fiancé, actually—she'd embraced a simpler style. Simple meaning Marlie no longer bothered with make-up, stuck her bushy, over-grown hair in a ponytail, and adopted yoga pants, a tank top, and flip-flops as her uniform. It wasn't as though she spent her days in pajamas, she thought virtuously. But that was only because she slept in her clothes.

So what? It was an efficient, time-saving system and there was nobody around to see her, except Ty, who didn't count.

He wouldn't have noticed anyway. But Axelle *had* noticed and that was the ouchy part. Axelle had forced Marlie to acknowledge that there was a difference between simple and unkempt.

The first time they'd met face-to-face, when Axelle had been bringing by the new menus for the downtown Houston restaurant she and her brother owned, Axelle's gaze had swept over Marlie, and her expression had immediately changed to concern.

"You should have told me you were sick!" Axelle had made little French tsking sounds. "We won't be using the new menus until next week, so updating the website can wait. Please. Return to bed. Get well."

"Okay" was all Marlie had been able to manage as Axelle had quickly backed out the door.

Marlie hadn't been sick. Or in bed.

After hurrying across the hall to the powder room beneath the stairs and really studying herself in the mirror for the first time in months, Marlie couldn't justify feeling insulted. Especially when Axelle returned later with leftovers from the restaurant, including veggies swimming in the most intensely flavored broth Marlie had ever tasted.

Axelle was explaining that her brother, the chef, had made it especially for Marlie when Tyler, who'd been lured downstairs by the smell of the food, appeared in the doorway.

At the sight of Marlie's housemate, Axelle had beamed a smile so bright it had dazzled Ty, who'd remained dazzled and smitten to the point of goofiness ever since.

Marlie was going to have to make this up to him somehow.

She stood by her office door several more minutes, just in case Ty and Axelle fell into a passionate clinch on the doorstep and needed the sofa again. Yeah. "Need the sofa" was going to be their new code for alone time. "Alone time" being code for doing the horizontal mambo. Which was—

The garage door opener cranked and a few moments later, Tyler's car engine started, interrupting Marlie's mental avoidance of the word *sex*.

Ty's car zoomed away. The garage door closed with a final "thunk" leaving Marlie in silence. It was weird because even though she hadn't heard them upstairs, the place seemed overly quiet now.

Marlie folded back the double doors of her office and took the three steps across the entryway that brought her to the foot of the stairs leading to the living area. She gazed up at the sound-absorbing carpet that had been her undoing. Ty and Axelle hadn't heard her approach and she'd been too preoccupied to notice the soft jazz playing.

Ty had wanted privacy for tonight—a perfectly reasonable request. Marlie climbed the stairs. The first time he'd brought a date home, Marlie had gone to a movie, but wasn't away long enough. The next time, she'd taken her old laptop, which she kept on hand for computer-crash emergencies, and hung out in her car in the garage. She'd enjoyed surfing the internet and posting on discussion boards. Unfortunately, she'd fallen asleep in her car and Ty had discovered her the next morning. He got points for being horrified even though she hadn't minded. Sure, she owned the townhouse, but he lived there, too, and was entitled to time alone. It wasn't his fault that she didn't have anywhere to go.

Reaching the top of the stairs, Marlie saw the remains of Ty's dinner for Axelle—bouillabaisse, bread and salad. She fixed her eyes straight ahead to avoid looking at the sofa, and made a beeline for the kitchen. Maybe there was still some soupy goodness in the pot on the stove. She lifted the lid. Score! Not only that, but a pastry box from Axelle's restaurant sat on the counter. Inside, Marlie saw two black and white wedges, their tops decorated with chocolate scrolls twining around one perfect raspberry. Ty and Axelle hadn't gotten around to dessert. Regretfully, Marlie closed the box and scooped a bowl of tepid soup, which she zapped in the microwave. Doing so toughened the chunks of seafood, but Ty wasn't here to protest that she was ruining his one and only impress-the-date specialty.

No, he wasn't here. She might have a problem. Marlie leaned against the counter and ate, all the while wondering if Ty was angry enough to move out. He would eventually, but construction on the townhouse he'd bought had been delayed because the developer had run into permit issues with the city. Marlie sent up a silent cheer for government bureaucracy and the extra time it gave her to build a financial cushion. If the delay was long enough, Ty would be the last renter she'd be forced to have in order to afford her mortgage.

He was a really excellent roommate. Because their parents were longtime friends, she knew his background, a major plus. And until a few months ago, he traveled so often for his job with an oil company that he wasn't around much.

Marlie tore off a hunk of bread and sopped the last of the bouillabaisse from the bowl. Yeah, the situation with Ty was as good as she'd ever find and she'd blown it because she'd been distracted.

He was really hung up on Axelle, who was the anti-Marlie. Axelle was French, for one thing, which gave her a sophistication Marlie could never equal, even when she was on her game. Axelle was also one of those women who always looked put together. Marlie suspected it was genetically impossible for her to look sloppy.

A little broth dribbled down Marlie's chin and onto her tank top. She set the bowl in the sink and dabbed at her chest with a paper towel. Perfect example. This would never happen to Axelle.

Tyler always went for the polished types. She guessed that he'd be shocked at the hours and expense Axelle invested in her ever-glossy appearance. It took time and money to keep up with manicures and facials and highlights and who-knows-what skin treatments and fitness classes. Axelle made an effort. Marlie didn't. Simple as that.

As she dropped the wadded paper towel into the trash can beneath the sink, Axelle's pastry box called to her. Technically, what was *in* the box was doing the calling. Marlie eyed it before surrendering and lifting the lid. Chocolate fumes made her momentarily light-headed. She couldn't simply help herself, although she really wanted to. On the other hand, it wasn't as though Tyler would eat both pieces.

Axelle probably wouldn't have eaten a piece. No elastic-waisted pants for her. She was the glamorously chic hostess of Ravigote, the restaurant she owned with her brother. She handled the business side as well, and Marlie knew for a fact that Axelle worked as many hours a day as she did. So, no, Marlie was not in any way jealous of Axelle.

Except for having unlimited access to fabulous desserts and clearly being able to resist their siren song. But that's what elastic was for, right?

Maybe she could cut a little from each wedge. Just a taste. While they were fresh. Choosing a long, sharp knife—one of the set Axelle had given Ty—Marlie carefully sliced a sliver from the side of one of the pieces. At least she thought she was carefully slicing, but the dessert had warmed, softening the cakey part, and the hard icing on top cracked when she pressed on it. The raspberry rolled down the side, leaving a pink trail. If the knife hadn't left an impression, Marlie would have stuck the box into the fridge and pretended not to know anything had happened.

Fine. She'd just eat the whole thing and if Ty objected, or

even noticed, she'd go buy him another piece. He probably wouldn't be back tonight, anyway.

Taking a bite from the point of the wedge, Marlie closed her eyes in sugary, chocolatey, bliss. Fabulous. Ravigote, serving Texas-European fusion cuisine—Marlie had made up that term—was out of her price range, so she enjoyed the samples that came her way now that Ty was dating Axelle.

The dessert was so rich that Marlie felt a little sick after eating it. "And that's what they call 'just desserts,'" she said aloud and laughed.

Oh. She looked down at her chocolatey fingers. "I'm telling myself jokes. Not a good development."

After putting the pastry box into the fridge, Marlie loaded the dishwasher and wiped the counter. She knew Ty would have, but it was her fault he wasn't here to do it.

She'd finished and had just clicked off the kitchen light when she heard the back door open and close. She hadn't locked it. Adrenaline shot through her. The clock glowing on the microwave display told her it had been less than half an hour since Ty had left. He couldn't be back already. He wouldn't have had time to do more than drop off Axelle and return. Barely enough time for a good-night kiss.

She hadn't heard his car enter the garage, but maybe it was because the water had been running in the kitchen sink. The living area's mood lighting stretched into the darkened kitchen. Stepping into a shadow, Marlie clutched the dish towel and had two thoughts at the same time: as a weapon, the towel wasn't going to do a whole lot, and the footsteps were climbing the stairs two at a time the way Ty always did. Usually when he came home, Marlie was working downstairs and heard them receding; it was odd hearing them coming toward her. Still, she exhaled in relief as his head became visible through the slats in the banister.

"Hey," he said when he saw her.

"Hey," she said back. Ooo, yeah. He was still angry, but he was trying to hide it from her as he walked toward the kitchen bar.

Dropping his keys in the ugly ceramic dish Marlie had made during a joint family vacation many summers ago, he nodded toward the empty dining table as he took off his jacket. "You didn't have to clean up."

"I know." Marlie folded the dishtowel over the rack. "But I figured I owed you and I had no idea when you'd be back." *Or if you'd be back.*

"It's not like I could stay over there." Ty's profile was to her as he looked across at the sofa. He still had eye shadow on his cheek.

Nope. Not gonna look at the sofa. "Because…?"

"Because she lives with her brother."

"I didn't know that. Since when?"

"Since the week we met." Ty draped his jacket over a chair. "Business is down and since Paul lives in a loft across the street from the restaurant, it made sense for Axelle to move in and take a smaller salary until things turn around."

"Very practical." If there was anything Marlie understood, it was needing a roommate to share expenses.

"And, look, I know we're all adults, but sound really carries in a loft and we're talking about the guy's *sister*—"

"Okay! Got it!" Marlie smiled brightly as Ty gave her a strange look. "I promise you that we can work this out. Just let me know when and I'll…I'll go stay in a motel somewhere."

Ty shook his head and walked past her to open the fridge. "You don't have to do that." The light illuminated his face as he stared inside.

Don't take out the box. Don't take out the box.

Thankfully, he grabbed a beer, twisted off the cap and took a long swallow, drawing Marlie's attention to his throat.

How many times had she seen him do just that? Not specifically drink a beer, but a bottle of water or an energy drink or
some other liquid? He'd open the container and immediately
take his first swallow standing by the refrigerator while the
door closed. Had she ever noticed his neck before? No. Why
would she notice Tyler Burton's manly neck, for pity's sake?
Why was she noticing it now?

He lowered the bottle and gave her a long look. Marlie
braced herself for the announcement that he was moving out.
Since she'd hung up the towel, she didn't have anything to do
with her hands, so she crossed her arms.

Tyler walked toward her, looking very predatory.

Marlie's heart thumped even harder than when she'd heard
the door earlier and thought someone was breaking in. Except
this wasn't fear; it was anticipation. But what *exactly* was she
anticipating?

Tyler moved across the room as though in slow motion,
his blue eyes steady, his cheek bones sculpted—but not in a
modelly way, in a manly way. He didn't smile. His lips looked
fuller when they weren't stretched in a smile. Very kissable
lips, as a matter of fact. Nice and smooth. Maybe he used
ChapStick to keep them in peak kissable condition.

Marlie might have some ChapStick around somewhere. It
wouldn't hurt her to swipe it over her mouth every so often,
if she happened to remember. Not as if she was going to get
kissed any time soon, she thought, staring at the mark on his
cheek. And then it sure wasn't going to be by somebody who
was wearing more eye shadow than she was.

Without breaking eye contact, Ty stopped in front of her,
not exactly in her personal space, but definitely close enough
to smell the chocolate on her breath.

His eyes narrowed slightly as he tilted the beer bottle and
took another long swallow.

Oh, he was getting ready to say something Marlie didn't

want to hear. In fact, he was probably thinking about how to break the bad news to her. Marlie clamped her lips together because she refused to beg. And because maybe then he wouldn't smell the chocolate.

TYLER LOOKED DOWN AT the woman who'd been sabotaging his love life since the summer between fourth and fifth grade.

He vividly remembered that summer. Their families had rented cabins in Colorado and enrolled Ty and Marlie in soccer camp. Marlie, being two years younger, practiced with the seven and eight year olds, while Ty was with the nine-tens, including dark-haired, dark-eyed, long-legged Blanca with the wicked kick. Blanca fascinated him—specifically her hair which blew all around, yet always fell smooth and gleaming back into place. And after practice, did Ty get to go with Blanca and the rest of the team and hang around the pool? No. Ty had to go over to the next field to collect little red-faced, sweaty Marlie with her bushy ponytail and walk her back to their cabin. Blanca never sweated.

Blanca could have been his first girlfriend. Could have, but wasn't, not with Marlie tagging along with him everywhere.

And every other year or so, his summer was interrupted by a trip with Marlie's family where he ended up responsible for her. Forget any possible summer romance. Even worse, while he was away, any girl he liked back home would find someone else to hang around.

The only good thing was that Marlie never got a crush on him, so they got along okay. And there was the one good summer, when he got his driver's license and they met the twins—a girl for him and a boy for Marlie, so she had somebody else to follow around. That was the only time he ever actually enjoyed one of the vacations.

A boy for Marlie. Somebody else to follow around.

Hmm. Maybe grown-up Marlie needed a boyfriend to follow around.

Ty studied her as he tilted the beer back. She wasn't his type, but she'd been engaged, so she was somebody's type. Or she had been. Her hair was still bushy—it kind of went with the eyebrows—but her face was pale and bland. Her eyes were wide as she watched him, arms hugging her torso, her hands disappearing into the sleeves of a gray hoodie she wore with baggy pants. She always wore a gray hoodie and baggy pants.

Depressed. The thought came to him and he wondered why he hadn't seen it before. She spent hours in her office dungeon staring at a computer screen. It was enough to make anybody depressed.

"You need to get out more," he told her.

She blinked and visibly relaxed.

What? Had she thought he was going to hit her or something? When had he ever threatened her? Sure, he'd been mad earlier, but that was mostly frustration and he was over it. Or as much as he would ever be over it.

"I know," she said. "And I've already promised you that next time, I'll find—"

"I meant, for you. You look like a mole."

Another blink. "I get out. What do you call running with you every morning?"

"We're running together?"

He raised his eyebrows and she held up her hands. "Okay, we leave at the same time. Give me a break. I'm still increasing my endurance."

"You need light, Mole Girl. It's dark outside then."

"That's because it's December."

And that was another thing. "Is it?" Ty looked all around. "Where?"

"What do you mean, where?"

"I couldn't help noticing the lack of holiday spirit around here."

When she gazed at him warily, he gestured with the bottle. "Over there is a two-story bay window with nothing in front of it."

"I like the uncluttered look."

"You can be uncluttered for the other eleven months of the year, but that spot is begging for a tree. Where's your tree?"

"Still growing, I guess."

"Same as last year?"

"Trees take a long time to grow."

Yeah, she was depressed all right. He should have noticed before now. "Why don't you decorate?"

"Because then I'd have to undecorate." She spoke with exaggerated patience.

"Well, yeah."

She stared at him, one of those I'm-dealing-with-a-crazy-person stares. "What kind of look is that?" he asked her. "It's a reasonable question."

"We both went home for Christmas last year," she reminded him. "Putting up a tree would have been a waste of time."

"We're not going anywhere this year. Our parents are doing that Christmas and New Year's cruise."

"So?"

Ty opened his mouth, but when he couldn't think of anything to say, he took another sip of beer.

Marlie's face suddenly cleared. "I get it. You and Axelle want to decorate for Christmas." She flapped a long sleeve at him. "Please. Go ahead. Knock yourselves out."

Ty hadn't thought of it, but a decorating date wasn't a bad idea. Hot cocoa with a shot of Kahlua, sugar cookies, the air conditioning set on low so there could be a fire in the fireplace, jazzy Christmas music playing, maybe those cinnamony candles burning, all the good feelings associated with the holidays… Ty was so caught up in the idea, he almost didn't notice that Marlie had turned away and was headed upstairs to her bedroom.

"Hey."

She stopped and looked down at him, no curiosity in her eyes. Not much of anything, actually. But then, he hadn't spent a lot of time looking at Marlie Waters. When they were younger, he'd never paid attention because he was usually irritated.

For the first time, he considered that she was probably equally annoyed to have been dumped on him during their summer trips. Kind of like the way he'd been dumped on her the past few months.

There was a thought he hadn't expected. This was her house after all; although it was so easy living here he tended to forget. Their moms had cooked up this scheme when he'd been transferred to Houston. At first, Ty had only contacted Marlie to be able to say he had, but once he'd seen all this empty space and she seemed okay with him staying here… but had she been? Okay with it? Had her mom pressured her? Was having him living here making her depressed?

As he looked up at her, he tried to remember if her expression had always been carefully blank and he was only noticing now because of the new vantage point, or if he should get her into therapy ASAP and find some place else to live.

She was waiting for him to say something.

"I appreciate you letting me stay here. I know it's been a lot longer than we thought it was going to be." He watched for a reaction, a clue to her thoughts.

"It's not a problem."

Nothing. "Yeah, but you can't buy your own furniture when I've got mine taking up all the room." He nodded toward the living area. His stuff looked great in there, but it was guy stuff—an overscale chocolate-brown sofa, a massive coffee table he liked to put his feet on, and the flat screen TV mounted on the wall. You could barely see Marlie's glass dining table and she'd moved her loveseat downstairs to her office. "If you want me to put it in storage, say the word."

"It's *fine*," she said with a hint of emotion. "Furniture shopping isn't in the budget, which is why if you weren't paying rent, I'd have to find someone else." She took a step and then added, "But don't feel obligated to stay here if it's not working for you."

She seemed sincere. "I *want* to stay here," Ty assured her. "It's a great location. Better than my house, assuming it ever gets finished."

"That's why I picked this place." She gazed into the distance. "How could I pass up a revitalized neighborhood in the heart of the city with a chance to build a brand-new home just the way I wanted?" Marlie looked around. "And now I have my dream house. I chose every fixture, the colors, the floors, the crown molding, the upgraded granite counter tops, the marble around the fireplace, the appliances, the vanities and tile and the rain head in the shower." Marlie's voice grew louder. "I looked at over a thousand door pulls to find just the right ones."

"And they're perfect." He'd never noticed them. Who paid attention to hardware?

She gripped the banister. "You see this maple? I chose this." She slowly caressed it.

"Gorgeous." Why hadn't he let her walk upstairs?

Marlie nodded dreamily. "The builder thought I wouldn't notice when he substituted oak, but I did and I made him redo our railings." She blinked and froze. "*My* railings," she corrected in a quieter voice. "My. Railings."

Oh, no. The broken engagement. No, no, no. Not going there. They'd never discussed it and there was no need to bring it up. If he did, he was in for tears and sobbing and wailing and who knows what hysteria.

Marlie's face had gone even paler and she seemed to shrink.

Say good-night he told himself. *Escape now.*

She white-knuckled her precious maple banister.

Ty groaned inwardly. What the heck, the night was already shot. He might as well man up and let her sob on his shoulder for a few minutes. "Marlie, my mom told me you'd been engaged, but she didn't know what happened."

"That's because *my* mother doesn't know what happened, so she couldn't tell yours." Her lip trembled. "*I* don't even know what happened."

And then, of course, she proceeded to tell him what happened.

2

"ONE MINUTE, I WAS WAITING for Eric in the reception area at the title company so we could close on the townhouse and the next, he got off the elevator and told me he *can't do this*."

Eric would be the ex, Ty surmised.

"*I* thought he meant he didn't have time right then because something…"

This was going to take more than a few minutes.

"…could have called me on my cell…"

Ty jiggled his beer bottle. Empty.

"…and he said 'any of this.' The house. The job. The wedding. It was too much. He felt pressured. How could he feel pressured?" She poked at her chest. "*I* was the one who ran around taking care of all the details. *I* met with the builder, *I* planned the wedding, I arranged for the movers. I even packed. All he had to do was *show up!*"

"Maybe that was the problem." Ty made the mistake of saying.

Marlie's eyes went huge.

He tried to explain, also a mistake. "Maybe he felt left out. Maybe he wanted to be more involved." Even as he spoke, Ty knew he was saying the wrong thing. Besides, what guy wanted to be *more* involved in wedding plans?

Marlie's response was to run up the stairs.

"Marlie!"

Hell. But only the first level. It was going to get worse. If she hadn't told her own mother the details of Eric bailing out on her, that meant she probably hadn't told anybody. She'd kept everything bottled inside for what? A couple of years? Tonight would be her first venting. It was going to be epic. He was looking at the fourth or even fifth level of hell for sure.

Ty set his empty bottle on the kitchen bar and followed Marlie upstairs all the way into her bedroom. He was going to drag the story out of her if it took all night. Then he'd have the fun of convincing her that It Was Over and time to move on with her life. If all went well, Marlie'd find another guy and hang around with him, and then Ty could finally, *finally* spend quality time with Axelle.

"Marlie—" And he broke off.

He'd never been in her bedroom. His room was down the hall to the left and there was no reason for him to go to her end. There was an unspoken understanding that they stayed out of each others' bedrooms, and the most he'd seen of hers was a chair by the window if she'd left her door open.

So that was why he was hit with the full force of the bed. At first, he didn't even realize it *was* her bed. The mattress was entirely enclosed in a ceiling-high, open-sided white box with a charcoal-gray interior and rounded corners. He moved closer and saw task lights, speakers and a control panel in the padded headboard. It extended upward to form a solid canopy housing a projector, and continued in one piece all the way down past the foot of the bed to the floor. The interior of the footboard was a screen that stretched the width of the bed.

He'd gone slack-jawed. "That's…is that…?"

"The European media bed that was in all the magazines? Not exactly." Marlie came to stand beside him. "I couldn't afford the real thing, so I had this one made."

Ty glanced at her. She sounded better. Calmer. His interest in the bed seemed a good distraction for the moment, so he checked out the upholstered interior and the headboard controls. "You designed this?"

"Not by myself. I talked to the carpenters who built the house and showed them pictures. I ended up bartering a website for the bed frame. And then the electrician got involved and he knew a man who installed sound systems and so on. It was a collaborative effort."

"Wow." Every guy's fantasy bed. Ty had lived here a year and a half and had no idea something like this existed down the hall. Even more intriguing, he'd lived a year and a half with a woman who not only allowed the thing in her bedroom, she figured out a way to make it happen. He would never have picked Marlie for the type to have a techno bed. As far as he knew, she spent most of her time in her office, anyway. "Just wow," he said, thinking Marlie had become a lot more interesting and that her ex was an idiot.

"The bed adjusts for when you want to watch the screen." Marlie pressed a button on the control pad in the headboard and elevated the side nearest him.

"Each side has its own controls?" Did his voice actually crack?

She nodded. "Go ahead. Try it."

Ty ignored the fact that he was climbing into Marlie's bed and stretched out. His feet weren't anywhere near the end of the mattress, which meant it was a custom size. "It's comfortable," he said, thinking of all the things he'd like to do in this bed.

"That's the idea."

"You'd think. But I've run across a lot of great-looking, uncomfortable furniture." Ty ran his hands along the side of the mattress. "Good thing you didn't skimp on the quality.

This mattress has probably had quite a workout." That didn't sound right. "From watching movies and…stuff."

Marlie's eyes met his in one of her bland looks before she picked up a remote control. Curtains whirred across the sides, blocking the light, leaving Ty cocooned in total darkness. A moment later an ocean scene appeared on the screen.

The camera had filmed from a vantage point on the bow of a sailing ship. He heard the waves, the sails flapping in the wind, ropes creaking. Surround sound. Unbelievable. Ty half expected mist to shoot from the canopy ceiling to complete the experience.

What an escape. Imagine coming home to this bed after work. It would be like going on vacation every night.

Relaxing, he stared at the screen as the view bobbed up and down. Up and down. Up and— "Marlie?"

He heard laughter and the image disappeared.

"Getting seasick?" The curtains drew back and Marlie grinned down at him, taking him back in time.

Today we get to go on a hike! Mom packed our lunches— peanut butter, the smooth kind. Come on! Get out of bed, Ty! If we're late, they'll leave without us.

And he'd said, *I don't want to go on a stupid hike,* even though he did, and *I hate peanut butter,* even though he didn't.

Marlie had stopped grinning then, which was what he'd wanted. Why should she be happy if he wasn't?

He didn't want that now. A smiling Marlie was better than a crying Marlie. Smiling looked good on her, gave her a friendly, comfortable vibe. If she smiled more often, it wouldn't take long for her to find another guy. "This is a seriously awesome bed," he complimented her. "I don't know why you'd ever leave."

"Food?"

"Have it delivered."

"Uh, the thing that happens after you eat food?"

Ty leaned over the side and checked the height of platform. "There's room for a bedpan under here."

"You're talking about a chamber pot, but still ewww."

He noticed something else while he was leaning over. "No way." Pressing on a panel, he released the latch and opened the door of a small refrigerator. At the moment, it held a single bottle of no-name water and a lot of potential. He looked up at Marlie. "You are a goddess. Men everywhere should fall to their knees and worship you."

Ty expected her grin to widen, not fade. "What?"

"This bed was my wedding gift to Eric," she said, her voice flat.

Eric seriously annoyed him. "What was he, nuts? This is the greatest bed in the history of beds. How could he leave this bed?" Too late, Tyler realized how that sounded. "You. I meant how could he leave you."

Her expression didn't change. She wasn't buying it. He wouldn't have, either. "Because…any woman who'd give a guy a bed like this…shouldn't be left." Seriously? That the best he could do?

"He never saw it."

"Well, there you go. If he'd—" A beat passed. "What I meant—"

"Are you trying to make me feel better, Ty?"

"Yes. But I am doing a crappy job of it."

"You are doing a spectacularly bad job of it, and yet you keep hanging in there."

"I should stop."

"No." She sat at the foot of the bed by the screen. "I find it oddly endearing."

She might as well have patted him on the head. "As long as it keeps you from going over the edge."

"I'm not near an edge," she said, sounding edgy.

"Are you kidding? You're sitting on it with your feet dangling over the side."

"You think I'm still hung up on Eric?" She rolled her eyes. "Oh, please."

"Then ditch the drama and finish telling me what happened."

"Why?"

"Because I want to know."

"No, you don't."

Did he truly want to know what caused Marlie's broken engagement? Marlie was a what-you-see-is-what-you-get kind of person. Not glamorous, but solid and reliable. A team player, not a diva. She had "wife" written all over her. A man didn't mess around with a woman like Marlie.

He studied her familiar, bare face and those eyes that met his with disconcerting directness. He could never lie to those eyes. No matter what he said or how he acted, those eyes saw the truth. Except, apparently, where her ex was concerned.

So, yeah. He wanted to know what happened. "Given our past, I can see why you'd think I wouldn't care. I didn't figure it was any of my business. But now, I'm making it my business."

She didn't say anything, but some of the hurt left her expression.

"I want to find out what he did to turn you into a hermit who never goes anywhere and doesn't have any friends."

"I have friends," she protested.

"Your online buddies don't count. I'm talking about living, breathing friends you see in person."

"They're back in Seattle where I left them when I quit my job and followed Eric here to Houston!"

A little temper there. "Make new friends." Anger was encouraging. Wasn't it one of the stages of grief? He was fuzzy on the order.

She glared at him. "This is about you getting the place to yourself so you can sleep with Axelle, isn't it?"

Busted. "That's blunt."

"But I'm right."

"If helping you get out of your rut benefits me, I'm not going to complain."

She smirked. "That's the Ty I know."

"Following a guy around—that's the Marlie I know." He sucked air between his teeth. "Ignore what I just said."

She didn't. "We were engaged."

"I was out of line. I apologize."

"Our parents *made* me stick with you!"

"I know. I'm sorry for the crack. Can we get past it?"

She gave him a sulky look. "You're not endearing anymore."

"Endearing's not my style. Fixing things is my style. C'mon, let's get this over with. Spill."

"You are *really* bad at sympathy."

"Do you want me to make a lot of 'oh, I'm so sorry' and 'poor little Marlie' noises, or do you want a guy's perspective on what was going through your ex's head?" Ty already had a solid theory. Two theories, but he hoped he was wrong about the second.

"I don't care what he was thinking," Marlie said. "I want to know what happened between kissing me goodbye that morning and walking out of my life at noon."

Ty had theories about that, too. "Did you ask him?"

"I was so shocked, I don't remember saying anything." Marlie drew her feet onto the bed. "The bed was a surprise." She gazed around the interior. "I'd arranged for the carpenters to install it while we were at the closing. Then afterwards, we were supposed to come here and christen it."

An image of Marlie and the unknown Eric flashed in Ty's head and his mind rebelled. "Too much information."

She tilted her chin. "And your love life with Axelle isn't?"

"Point taken." He gestured. "Go on."

"I only told you so you'd understand that I was completely blindsided. He'd never complained or expressed any doubts. About anything. When Eric left for work that morning, everything was fine. Then he got off the elevator at lunchtime and gave his 'I can't do this' speech. He told me he felt tied down. He didn't like his job and he didn't like Houston, and apparently he didn't like me, either."

"He said that?"

Marlie gave him a look. "He called off the wedding. It's implied."

"Did he ask for the ring back?"

Marlie shook her head.

"So he didn't leave you for another woman," Ty said, glad that theory was toast.

"How do you know?"

"He would have wanted the ring so he could reset the stone or trade it in." At least Ty hoped Marlie had the sense not to hook up with a guy who was the type to give the same ring to another woman.

"Oh." She thought for a moment. "Is that supposed to make me feel better about being dumped?"

"It makes me feel better," Ty said. "Now I know we're only dealing with rejection and not betrayal." Betrayal was messier. Lots of crying and runny noses with betrayal. "If there had been another woman, you would have found a way to make the breakup all your fault. You would have blamed yourself for not being pretty enough or thin enough or whatever enough. Then you would have tried to fix yourself and punished the next guy you dated for being attracted to the 'new you' because he's supposed to be able to see past the 'new you' to the 'real you' hidden inside. But he doesn't know that. So you accuse him of being shallow. And then you break up with him—but not until he's wined you and dined you and paid for a couple of pricey bed-and-breakfast weekends."

"Not that you're bitter."

Ty so clearly spoke from experience that Marlie wanted to laugh. She actually felt like laughing. Maybe she would. "I hope she was good in bed, at least."

He met her eyes before giving her a rueful look. "She was okay. Tried too hard."

"Poor you." She snickered. It felt good. For the first time, Marlie experienced something other than bewildered hurt and anger when she thought about the horrible day Eric left. And who would have thought she'd be confiding in Ty, of all people?

Astoundingly, he seemed to care. Sure, it was self-serving, but it was genuine caring. And the clunky way he tromped all over her feelings might be just what she needed. She wasn't ready to admit it, though. He was smug enough already.

"Go ahead and laugh," he said. "But be glad you're not That Woman. At least you know Eric's issues had nothing to do with you."

Did she know that?

Ty settled back into the bed. Marlie wondered what he'd say if she told him he was the first man to be in it. But she didn't wonder enough to tell him.

"So he calls off the wedding and then what?" he prompted while he fiddled with the control panel, figuring out which buttons controlled the head elevation and the lights.

"He told me to keep his half of the down payment on the townhouse to cover the deposits I'd lose by canceling the wedding." Marlie thought of what she went through and got mad all over again. "Like that even began to make up for it. We were within sixty days of the date. The invitations hadn't been mailed, but they'd been printed. My dress had already been altered. The bridesmaids' dresses couldn't be returned and I couldn't make my friends pay for those, so I reimbursed them. Everybody had bought their plane tickets—"

"Focus," Ty cut her off. "What else did he say?"

"He just said 'sorry' and got back on the elevator."

"I mean, later. After that."

"There was no later," Marlie told him. "I haven't seen or talked to him since. No text, no email. Nothing."

"That was it?" Ty stopped playing with the buttons and stared at her. "You're kidding."

"No," she whispered, her throat tight. That was probably the most difficult aspect for her to accept—that Eric could walk away as though their life together had never existed.

"Jerk." Ty looked outraged. "What about his stuff?"

She swallowed past the tightness. "The movers told me he packed his car. He knew I had a couple of appointments that morning before I was to meet him at the title company and he must have come back after I left."

"So the coward planned it all in advance." Ty was gratifyingly incensed on her behalf. It helped.

"I thought it was stress. I thought he was having a meltdown and he'd get over it in a few hours. I mean, it happens. Even I— Anyway, they called me in for the appointment and what was I supposed to do? We had to vacate the apartment. The movers were already loading the truck. I had nowhere else to go. This was supposed to be our home. So I bought it. I went in and signed the papers and I bought it. Not that moment, because the papers had to be redone, but I moved in and paid the bank rent for a few days." Marlie breathed deeply, just as she had after walking into the room and indenturing herself to a mortgage.

"I would have done the same thing." Ty leaned over the side of the bed. "I'm going to drink your water." He opened the fridge, took the bottle she'd forgotten was in there, and twisted the cap.

Marlie smiled as he drank while the door clicked shut. He looked good in the bed. Very much at home. Nice broad shoulders, the kind she could rest her head on after he'd thrown an arm around her while they watched a movie.

Marlie thought all kinds of warm, fuzzy thoughts until the rational part of her pointed out that she was fantasizing about Tyler Burton.

It's only because he's here and he's male, she told herself. *You do not want Tyler Burton in particular; you want a man in general.*

Ty lowered the bottle. "How long did it take you to figure out he wasn't coming back?"

"A couple of days. He wouldn't answer his cell phone and I had visions of him lying in the hospital in a coma. I went by his work and they told me that he'd quit to take a job overseas." Yeah. His coworkers had to tell her. An echo of the humiliation she'd felt reverberated through her. "*Overseas?* Like any country would do as long as it was on a different continent than the one I was on?"

"Marlie." Ty leveled a look at her. "Drama free."

No coddling from Ty, which was probably the only reason she was able to get through her story without crying. "I just couldn't believe it. He'd never said anything about wanting to live in another country. Why didn't he ask me? I would have been up for it."

"Do I really have to answer that?" Ty asked. "Do I really have to tell you it was because he didn't want you to go with him?"

"That's cold."

"Marlie!" He looked pained. "This cannot be news to you. Forget about it. You went to his office—he wasn't there, then what?"

Marlie skipped the part about crying for hours after discovering he'd put her name on the "block personal information" list at his new company. As if she was a stalker. "I called his mom, who, by the way, was under the impression that Eric had bought me this house as a lovely parting gift. I set her straight on that, as well as what it was going to cost to cancel the wedding."

"Details I don't need."

Marlie exhaled in frustration before continuing, "She expressed her opinion. I expressed mine."

Ty gave her a thumbs up.

"And she refused to tell me where he was. Not even what country he was in."

"You're not looking too good here," Ty said.

Marlie's jaw dropped. "*I'm* not?"

"You're the one who fell in love with that turkey."

"I didn't know he was a turkey."

"We'll work on your turkey-detecting skills after I fix this problem," he said.

"Other than a really large mortgage and a really small income, I don't have a problem."

"Yes, you do." Ty sipped more water. "You're not over him yet."

"Oh, I'm over him. But I don't know how I missed the signs that something was wrong."

"Hey. Listen to me." Ty leaned forward, holding her gaze intently. "There weren't any signs. He made sure of it because he wanted out. Confronting you in public, breaking your heart, and taking away your dream home was calculated to make you hate him."

Marlie believed him. She didn't want to, but she knew Ty was giving her the unvarnished truth. "But why?" It was the question she'd asked herself way too many times. If Ty could answer it, he was a genius.

"Because then you wouldn't want him back. No hoping you could 'work things out.' It would be a clean break and you both could move on. Like ripping off a bandage. It stings, but it doesn't hurt for as long."

"It was a lot more than a sting."

"For you, yes. But he'd been planning his move for a while. He'd already checked out of the relationship. You don't do what he did to somebody you love."

Unvarnished truth hurt. "You're saying he'd fallen out of love with me?"

Ty nodded.

"But he, but we still—"

"That would be him hiding the signs."

"Did he have to hide them twice just the night before?"

"He was being thorough," Ty said implacably.

Details from their last night together flooded her memory. "We talked about our future that night. We talked about having *children*." Marlie swallowed. "I feel sick."

"Now, if you had a bed pan in here, we'd be all set."

She stared at Ty. "You are unbelievable. How can you say such a thing? He broke my heart and you act like it was nothing more than a broken date. Don't you have any empathy at all?"

Ty offered her the water bottle.

"I don't want any water!"

"Still feel sick?" He tilted the bottle to his mouth.

"I'm too mad at you to feel sick. Oh." She watched him, or rather she watched his neck as he drained the water. "You made me angry on purpose. I suppose you think that was clever."

"Yeah. I'm getting better at this."

"You're getting lucky."

"That is *not* what I'm getting."

"Aaaand we're back to that."

"I never left."

As much as Marlie wanted to be mad at him, she wasn't. Ty was blunt and sometimes annoyed with her, but he was here and he'd never lied to her.

Marlie suddenly looked back on all those summers in a different light. He'd hated having to be responsible for her and yet, not once had he failed to show up when he was supposed to. He hadn't taken it out on her, either. Sure, he obviously resented babysitting her, but other than that, they were friends. Just not friends who liked each other. Ty was the kind of friend who told her the truth because she needed to hear it and he didn't care how it made him look.

He screwed the top back on the empty bottle. "Okay, here's what happened with Eric."

Good, Marlie thought. *Finally I'll know.*

"He took one of those overseas jobs for single guys."

"Why do they have to be single?" Because women were involved? Marlie tried to imagine Eric as a sort of exotic male escort. No. Now Ty…

"It's common in the oil business. Some countries don't allow foreign women and children to live there, so companies recruit unmarried men. That way, they're not separating families. It's less complicated all around. The deal is you sign a contract for a year or two years, work twelve hour days and live in on-site corporate housing."

"You're saying he'd rather do that than marry me?"

"It's the cash," Ty said. "You make a pot full. I've seen these guys when they come back stateside after finishing a contract. They party hard and throw a lot of money around. They get the flashy cars and the flashy women and it looks pretty sweet, especially when you're stuck in a cubicle earning a lot less and about to take on a wife and mortgage."

"Eric proposed to *me,*" Marlie clarified. "*He* is the one who asked me to quit my job and move halfway across the country with him."

Ty nodded to himself. "Now what he did really makes sense."

"Not to me."

"Say I'm Eric." Ty paused. "Do I look like him?"

"You look exactly like him," Marlie said, and then watched the emotions flicker across Ty's face. She added a gooey look and saw the beginnings of panic. Good. He was entirely too smug. "Except that Eric's hair is dark and curly. And his eyes are brown." She touched her chin. "He had a beard thing here and he wore glasses. He might have been a *little* chunkier than you, not that he was out of shape, but he was buying the relaxed-fit Dockers, if you know what I mean. But you two could be twins. *From different families.*"

"You could have said no."

"Where's the fun in that?"

A slow smile slid across his face. "You'll be okay."

Marlie had not been the direct recipient of such a smile from Tyler. It warmed her middle and caused her heart to give a few syrupy thuds. *Remember that he reconnected your buttons. Just don't connect with him.* She poked his foot with hers. "Keep channeling Eric."

"Right. Eric." Ty gazed up at the canopy. "So I'm Eric and these guys head out for drinks and whatever, but I can't go because I have to taste wedding cake samples with Marlie and her mom and her girlfriends."

"It was just me, you were late, and you'd been drinking beer, so none of the cakes tasted good to you."

Ty looked at her. "For real?"

"Yes."

"You were mad."

"Well, yeah." Eric had embarrassed her in front of the other couples who'd been there.

"When I told the guys, they gave me a hard time about being on a leash."

"A leash?"

"Words to that effect." Ty waved his hand. "There were more instances like that and I started thinking the 'if onlys.' If only I weren't getting married. If only I could take a year or two and make some big bucks and buy the kind of car I really want, go where I want and do what I want. If only I didn't have to follow Marlie around to caterers and florists and invitation makers—"

"I didn't bother you with any of that. And I thought it would be fun to taste a bunch of cakes. You like cake."

"Marlie, work with me." Ty gave her an impatient look. "It's not the details. I'm showing you his frame of mind and how he got there. While you were all involved with the wedding and the house, he was seeing a really great life pass him by. These guys had money and freedom and no responsibilities. What would he have? Kids and a giant mortgage."

"He'd have me," she said in a small voice.

"But you wouldn't be you—you'd be a mother."

"Of his children!"

Ty spread his hands. "I'm telling you the way a guy thinks."

Truly, it was like watching a special feature on a DVD, the one where the director explained different scenes. "That's the way all guys think?"

"Nah. Some guys are into it."

"Is that the way you think?" It would explain why he never dated the PTA mom type.

Ty considered her question. "I'm in the middle—buying a house, but definitely not ready for a wife and kids." He regarded her with a touch of sympathy. "He wasn't ready, either, Marlie. You need to find a guy who's ready."

She'd thought she had. "Why didn't he just tell me?"

"He felt guilty after dragging you halfway across the country."

"I would have waited for him."

"And he knew that." Ty shook his head. "I hate to say it, but the guy actually did the decent thing. He just didn't expect you to mope about it for so long."

Men always stuck together in the end. "I'm not moping. I'm *working*."

"Then you're moping while you work." He eyed her before swinging his legs over the side of the bed. "This is a great bed." He leaned on his hands as he scanned the interior. "Too bad you have to get rid of it."

3

"WHAT? WHY?" MARLIE asked.

Ty's jaw hardened. "Because every time you come in here, you see it and think of your ex and what he did."

And Marlie knew he was right.

"You don't enjoy this bed. You hardly spend any time in here. Half the nights you fall asleep on the loveseat in your office."

He knew? He would have had to come downstairs specifically to check on her. While she was sleeping. Her breath hitched. "I work late."

"Because you're avoiding the bed. You never would have chosen this bed for yourself and it will always remind you of a wedding that didn't happen. Stop punishing yourself for something that wasn't your fault and ditch the bed."

"I can't afford to."

"Sell it," Ty said, and Marlie knew he wasn't going to let up until she agreed. "You know you could in about thirty seconds. Sell it to me. I'll give you whatever it cost you. There. Done. Problem solved." He looked pleased with himself.

Except... "It won't fit in your room."

"It'll fit in my new house."

"Which isn't finished," she reminded him.

"It's getting there," he said. "I meant to tell you, the city inspectors signed off on the new street plans and the council approved them this week. I drove by and crews are already replacing sewer pipes and widening the roads. The builder says once that's finished, it'll only be six weeks until I can move in."

Sooner than she'd thought. But the road wasn't finished yet. Besides, it was December and construction always slowed down in December. "So until then, your plan is to leave the bed here?"

Ty stared longingly at the screen behind Marlie. "I'll put it in storage."

That could work, but Marlie didn't know if she was ready to handle the thought of Axelle and Ty having sex in her wedding present to Eric. "Actually, the carpenters have dibs if I sell it."

"There's no 'if.' You're going to sell it."

Ty was right. *Somebody* should have sex in her wedding present to Eric. "I'll check to see if they're still interested."

"Do it." Ty exhaled heavily. "But I wish you'd told me before I bonded with the bed. I had great things planned for this bed."

"So did I."

They sat in silence. Marlie thought about how long it had been since she'd had great things, and then she thought about Ty and his plans for the bed. He was probably great at things, and she already knew the bed was great, so naturally she wondered about great things with Ty in the bed, but Eric kept creeping into her thoughts. Marlie realized it would be impossible for her to have great things in this bed. Ever.

"I'm calling the carpenters tomorrow," she said at the same time Ty said, "I can't buy your bed."

"I thought you wanted it," she said.

He looked at her accusingly. "I know the story. That means

every time I'm in this bed, I'll think of you. It would be distracting at certain crucial times."

"Sorry." But she really wasn't.

He exhaled. "If the carpenters want it, tell them to haul it off right away. As soon as the check clears, go bed shopping. You need a bed that's you." He ran his hand over the frame. "This was never you."

How did he know that? "What kind of bed do you think is me?"

"Unbleached cotton, a thick comforter, squashy pillows," he said immediately. "Beach colors. No patterns because you want to rest your eyes. Maybe a four poster, but nothing heavy. You need a bedside table with a soft light and a CD player where you can play New Age relaxation music."

Marlie had expected him to say something like "blue" or "traditional."

He was on a roll. "Get a good mattress that will support your back so it won't get sore from sitting all day. No computer outlets. *Maybe* a TV across the room, but I'd say no. You need an electronic-free zone."

"Okay," Marlie said, dazzled with the details and amazed that he'd described her perfect bedroom before she even knew it was her perfect bedroom. Except for the New Age music.

He stood and looked around. "If you want to paint in here, I'll help."

"Okay," she said again. He was being awfully nice. She tried not to be suspicious.

"It's late." He flexed his shoulders, drawing his shirt across his chest and she thought, *his chest is nice, too.* "Get some sleep."

It will be a while, Marlie thought as she stood. "Thanks. And, again, I'm sorry about ruining your dinner."

He looked down at her. "Want to make it up to me?"

"Yes," she said before finding out what he had in mind.

"Get a Christmas tree."

That was not what she hoped he had in mind. But he wouldn't think that way about her. She wasn't his type. And as soon as she tightened up her current date requirements to being beyond male and breathing, she'd remember he wasn't her type, either.

"A tree is easy enough." Marlie thought of the little pre-decorated table top trees. She could order one online.

"'Easy' means you're thinking of some wimpy thing. I'm talking about a big tree for the front window."

"Oh, come on."

He headed for the door. "Those are my terms."

His *terms?* "Or what?"

He stopped at the doorway and grinned evilly. "Or I will call your mother and tell her I'm worried about you."

Marlie gasped.

"I'll tell her all you do is work and the stress is getting to you."

"Oh, that's low, Ty."

"*And* I'll say that I suspect you've never gotten over your broken engagement and you're depressed—which might be true."

"It's not true," Marlie insisted.

"Convince me. Get a tree."

"Okay! I'll get a tree. Is pre-lit okay, or do you have rules about that, too?"

"*Pre-lit?*" Ty looked as though she'd suggested serving one of Santa's reindeer for Christmas dinner. "You're talking about an artificial tree?"

"Well, yeah."

He stared at her.

"My house, my tree," she said. "Do not call my mother."

"Okay. I won't call your mother. I'll call *my* mother. All I have to say is that you're not yourself and I'm concerned about what will happen when I'm not here to check on you."

Marlie's blood ran cold.

"And you know if your mom hears about it from my mom, it'll be ten times worse."

"It would be a thousand times worse." Marlie had visions of her parents canceling their cruise and arriving on her doorstep. "You win. I'll get a tree. A giant, needle-dropping, fire-hazard of a tree."

Ty hadn't said anything about ornaments.

THE NEXT DAY, MARLIE received flowers from Axelle. Before noon. Which meant Ty must have gone straight from blackmailing Marlie over the Christmas tree to discussing her with his girlfriend.

Good times.

Marlie held the heavy, square glass vase and searched her office for an empty flat surface. Eventually, she had to clear off the top of a file cabinet and set the exotically chic arrangement there, where she could see it while looking up the names of the flowers on Google. They were bright, beautiful and out of the ordinary. Like Axelle.

Not a carnation, rose or daisy in the bunch. Like Marlie. If she hadn't gone to seed.

If anyone should have been sending flowers, it should have been Marlie, but now that Axelle had outclassed her, Marlie had no choice but to dig out her good stationery, ordered for her wedding thank-yous, and write a charming, lively note to Axelle.

Charming and lively did not come naturally to Marlie, so writing the note took some time. She was not helped by staring at her given name, Marlene, written across the top of the stationery. Her mother had insisted on it, just as she'd insisted that Marlene be on the wedding invitations. They'd never looked quite right to Marlie, as though it was someone else marrying Eric. And look how that turned out.

She had to access the U.S. Post Office website to find out what a first-class stamp cost these days, and then walk down to the mailbox cluster at the end of the block and drop it in the slot.

No wonder people emailed everything.

WHEN TYLER ARRIVED HOME that evening, the bed was leaving. He felt a pang, because it was a stupendous bed, but it came with baggage and Ty didn't need baggage. To be honest, he was still a little freaked that he kept picturing Marlie when he thought of the bed. Adult Marlie was bad enough, but as he was mentally planning an evening with Axelle, the Marlie that had intruded was the eight-year-old Marlie. He couldn't help it. Even now, when he thought of Marlie, her sweaty little red-cheeked face came to mind. It was the ponytail. Marlie may have changed, but the messy, bushy lump hadn't. Ty just couldn't have sex in a bed he associated with an eight-year-old.

Marlie had moved fast. Four men were dismantling the frame and carrying pieces downstairs to a pickup truck. Ty stepped aside as two of them passed him carrying the screen that had been at the foot of the bed.

He consoled himself with the thought that he would have replaced the projection system with a flat screen anyway. Newer technology.

Marlie was in her office—no surprise. Except that she seemed remarkably sanguine about getting rid of a bed she'd kept as a shrine to a failed romance.

Ty leaned against the doorway. Marlie wore headphones and didn't see him at first. A bouquet of bright flowers partially obscured her from view. He waved a hand so the movement would attract her attention.

She saw him and removed the headphones as she raised her eyebrows. "What's up?"

She looked the same as always, maybe faintly curious, since it wasn't his habit to interrupt her when he came home. He seemed more affected by last night's discussion than she was.

"The bed." He hooked a thumb over his shoulder. "I guess the carpenters wanted it."

"Yeah. They couldn't get here fast enough. I don't think they've decided who gets to take it home, though."

"Did you go shopping for a new one?"

"I haven't had time." She indicated the arrangement of colorful exotic blooms that she'd set on a file cabinet. "Your girlfriend sent me flowers."

Ty smiled. "She's great like that." Axelle's impulsive generosity was one of the things that attracted him to her. It was also how she'd ended up in charge of the Midtown Business Mentors Charity Auction this Friday. And how he'd been corralled into helping. And how Marlie had ended up doing a website for them. It was difficult to say no to Axelle.

"I broke out my expensive wedding stationery and wrote her a thank-you note for the 'day brightener.'" Marlie looked at him. "I wonder where she got the idea that I needed a 'day brightener?'"

"You mind that I told her about your jerk of a fiancé?" he asked. "You've got nothing to be ashamed of."

"I'm not ashamed, but it was almost three years ago," Marlie said. "I'm more embarrassed about walking in on you last night and seeing Axelle half-naked."

"You said your eyes were closed."

"They were. *After* I saw you both."

Ty drew a long breath. "*I* should have sent *her* flowers."

"You're in luck," Marlie said. "As it happens, I've got some right here."

"I'm not going to take your flowers."

"Why not? I feel I owe her."

"She'd rather have you do a little extra on the auction website."

"It would be cheaper to send her flowers." Marlie nodded toward the computer screen. "They've had twice as many donations as Axelle anticipated. Each one means I have to put up a picture and a description and a link to the company or person who donated it," she told him. "I'm setting the whole thing up so I can stream the auction and take online bids Friday night. It's taking a little more time than I'd estimated."

Ty came over to look at the screen. "It's for a good ca—what the heck is that?"

"That," Marlie said, "is why I don't mind the extra time."

A shirtless man wearing suspenders and a fireman's hat grinned at him from the monitor. "What's he donating?"

"A date," Marlie answered.

"Did he have to look like he was posing for a calendar?"

"Actually, he did. You're looking at Mr. May." She smiled. "And I'm sure the lucky winner hopes he will."

Ty raised his eyebrows.

Marlie typed a caption to the picture and then read it aloud. "Oh, yeah. I'd like to see the partridge in *his* pear tree."

"Uh, Marlie?"

"Hmm?" The picture on the screen changed and another man appeared. This one was wearing more clothes, but his smile promised he wouldn't be wearing them long. Ty had a passing acquaintance with that smile and a guy shouldn't *ever* be photographed smiling that smile.

"And you can coo in my ear anytime." Marlie typed "Two Turtle Doves."

"What are you doing?"

"This is the 12 Men of Christmas Dating Extravaganza."

"Is it legal?"

Marlie laughed. "Axelle found twelve men to agree to take the winners or winner on a date inspired by verses from 'The Twelve Days of Christmas' song." She typed as she spoke.

"Axelle didn't ask me," Ty said, wondering how Axelle knew the men.

"Axelle doesn't want to share you," Marlie told him.

"Or she doesn't think anyone would pay to go out with me."

"More likely, she's afraid you'll embarrass the other guys by starting a bidding war."

Ty liked the sound of that. It could happen. He envisioned hordes of women emptying their bank accounts and shouting bids faster than the auctioneer could keep up.

And then he noticed Marlie looking at him with her all-seeing gaze. He gestured with his chin toward the computer screen. "How high does Axelle think women will bid to go out with these men?"

"I have no idea," Marlie told him. "But there's a minimum bid of six hundred dollars."

"Fifty bucks a date? What a deal. You can barely go to the movies and get popcorn, drinks and a pack of Junior Mints for fifty bucks."

"I don't fix the starting bids. I just put up the auction items. But I think the low minimum is because this is offered as an all or nothing package," Marlie explained. "Axelle said some of the guys were afraid no one would bid on them. This was the only way they'd agree to participate. She's encouraging women to form buying cartels and split up the guys among them."

He nodded. "In case anyone is too shy to bid by herself. Good idea. So show me the men's package."

Marlie slowly turned her head and looked up at him.

"I meant," Ty said, feeling irritated, "are there women for sale?"

"You meant that, did you?"

"Is there a women's version of the dating dozen?" he asked heavily as Marlie continued typing, visibly fighting a grin.

"No—ooolala, Mr. Three French Hens. I wonder if *French* is his specialty."

Ty looked at the screen. *That's Axelle's brother!*

"So *that's* Paul." Marlie propped her chin on her elbow as she zoomed in. "Mmm." She traced his lips with the cursor and then zoomed in even more until just his mouth and square chin with the cleft filled the screen.

How did he shave that thing, anyway? Ty wondered. Judging by the dreamy expression on Marlie's face, that was not what she was wondering. Sighing, she zoomed out. "I'm glad Axelle has no problem sharing *him*."

Ty looked at her in concern. Now that he'd helped her get over Eric, she wasn't going to go wild, was she? The idea was to find an area between nun and nymphomaniac.

The next photo popped up. "Four calling birds. Call me anytime." Her voice dropped to a sexy purr.

"You do know it's actually 'colly' birds." Ty sounded uptight and condescending. He always sounded uptight and condescending when he was losing control of a situation. *There is nothing here to control,* he told himself.

"Why, Tyler." Marlie looked up at him and mercifully away from the lumberjack Jo in his unbuttoned flannel shirt. "I do know that, but I'm amazed that *you* do."

"I took chorus for my Fine Arts credit in college," he said, condescendingly. *Stop that.*

Mr. Five Gold Rings appeared. "A gymnast?" The photo had been taken during a competition. The man's arm muscles bulged as he suspended himself by the ring apparatus.

"Look at that form," Marlie said with admiration. "And gymnasts are so flexible."

Ty waited. "Aren't you going to say 'he can run rings around me' or something like that?"

"I was thinking that if he's that good with two rings, he'll be spectacular with five. That's golden."

"What does that even mean?"

"Mmm." Marlie smiled a little smile as she typed.

Ty felt out of his depth, a totally foreign feeling. Depth like this was supposed to be his specialty.

"This next guy is all about laying."

Of course he was.

Marlie clicked the mouse to bring up the next photo. Sure enough, there was a guy holding a goose. Shirtless. The man, not the goose. Though technically, the goose was already shirtless. "Axelle found these guys?" Ty's voice was pitched higher than normal.

"Yes. Isn't it great?"

Ty deliberately relaxed his throat. "Couldn't she have found anyone with a hobby requiring clothes?"

"You mean like a sports uniform?"

"Yes." Ty thought about baseball. "Exactly."

Marlie brought up the next picture. "Behold. Seven Swans a Swimming." She glanced up with mock innocence. "Check out the uniforms."

Speedos. Speedos worn by men with no body fat. Or modesty. "The entire swim team?"

"No," Marlie said, her voice regretful. "Just him." She cropped the other men out and enlarged the remaining swimmer, not that he needed enlarging, a point amply made by the skin-tight suit. "But he's enough, don't you think?"

"Yes. Plenty." Which one of them had been afraid no one would bid on him? Sheesh. Ty didn't lack for self-confidence, but these guys were enough to make him add another mile to his morning run.

"And he's a breast stroke champion. I should put that in the caption."

"Marlie." Tyler began to sweat. He'd never seen this side of her. He didn't know she had this side. She should keep this side to herself. He didn't want to be responsible.

He wasn't responsible, was he?

"What?"

Eight maids a milking was up next and Ty could only imagine. "How is it possible for you to make 'The Twelve Days of Christmas' sound smutty?"

"Smutty?" Marlie looked the picture of offended virtue. "Tyler, these men are donating their time in an effort to raise money for a program that provides a positive activity for underprivileged youth when they're most vulnerable to bad influences. What exactly do you find smutty about that?"

"I—"

"Furthermore, I've been posting all these auction items and I've yet to see what you've donated. Don't you support the business mentors program?"

"I donated you," he said.

Marlie blinked. "Excuse me?"

He gestured to the screen. "I suggested you for the website, since you do Axelle's restaurant already."

Marlie's eyes narrowed. "You mean I do the work and you get the credit?"

How did he end up the bad guy, here? "I'm covering the expenses for the site and your fee after the discount."

"Oh." She looked back to the screen. "I'd like to tell you to forget about my fee, but I need the money."

"No problem. You've put in a lot of hours and it wasn't really your cause to begin with." Or his, but that didn't mean it wasn't worthwhile. "You should find a cause. Volunteering would be a good way for you to interact with people." And by people, he meant men. And by interact, he meant talking in a controlled setting that was not a bar.

"I'm volunteering right now." Marlie had flipped into her photo editing program and was removing background clutter from the crop of the swimmer. "And I am so interacting." She zoomed in on his head and removed the red rings his goggles had left around his eyes. "There. Not that anyone is going to be looking at his face."

Ty hadn't known Marlie was so visual. "I meant interacting in person."

"I'm all for that." She sighed at the picture.

"Then volunteer for something other than computer work," Ty said. "Something that gets you out of the house." He got an idea. "In fact, why don't you come with Axelle and me to the auction on Friday? You'll get a chance to see everything first hand." And maybe Axelle could set her up with someone. Axelle knew everyone. Yeah, they could introduce Marlie to as many men as possible. One of them was bound to ask her out. Brilliant. *Tyler Burton, you are brilliant.*

Marlie's ponytail brushed against his arm and he looked down. She had an appealing casual vibe, but maybe Axelle could give her some tips about her hair before Friday. Figure out a way to contain it. Maybe lend her some lip gloss.

"I can't go," Marlie said. "We're streaming the auction live, remember? I have to monitor it from here."

Too bad. He'd practically had her married off.

"I'll get to see everything Friday afternoon when Randy and I set up the webcams."

"Randy?"

"Computer geek." Marlie clicked through to Nine Lords a Leaping.

A guy in a black Dominion of Zartha T-shirt posed against a stone wall, crossed arms displaying biceps not normally associated with computer geeks. At least he was clothed.

"He'll have a laptop down front at the auction. Our computers will be networked so I can control the webcams from here and Randy will be able to relay the online bids to the auctioneer."

"Axelle," Ty supplied.

"She decided to do it herself?" Marlie made a sound. "I thought she was going to ask someone else." Her eyes met his.

"Me?"

Marlie shrugged. "She wasn't specific."

Axelle had never come out and asked him. Had she expected Ty to offer to be the auctioneer? "I've never done anything like that before. This is a big deal. She should have gotten someone with experience."

"Whatever."

Did Axelle feel that he'd let her down? It was hard to figure out what she was thinking or wanted from him.

Marlie turned back to the computer. "By the way, she's coming here to change clothes before the auction. It'll save you a trip to pick her up."

"Sounds good." At least Axelle would be able to introduce Marlie around during the afternoon before people got dressed up. A casual setting was more Marlie's style, anyway.

There was a knock on the door jamb and one of the carpenters stuck his head in. "We've got it all, Marlie. We patched the holes where the brackets held the frame to the wall. I'd give it a day to dry before you paint over it."

"Okay."

"And thanks again!"

She gave a distracted wave and he let himself out.

"You're taking this very well," Ty said. "Where are you going to sleep tonight?"

"Mmm?"

"You don't have a bed."

"In here." She stared at the monitor. "On the loveseat."

She had to be working on Eight Maids a Milking. He couldn't help it. Ty looked at the computer screen where a man wore a milk mustache, his arms crossed over a beefy chest, if one could mix food groups. Enough already.

As Ty left, he heard Marlie sigh as the keyboard clicked. "Milk. It does a body really, really good."

4

WHEN AXELLE AND TY CAME downstairs dressed for the auction, Marlie was glad, glad, glad she couldn't go with them. Even she, who had the barest passing acquaintance with fashion, could tell that Axelle's simply-draped, one-shoulder, floor-length gown was wickedly expensive.

As for Ty, Marlie's preference for men in jeans changed right then and there—Ty in formal wear was something to behold.

Classic, elegant—two traits she hadn't fully appreciated before—and drop-dead handsome—which she'd definitely fully appreciated—he managed to stun her speechless.

It's basically a black suit, she told herself. A bunch of fabric. But that fabric broadened his shoulders, narrowed his waist and lengthened his legs. There was a lot to be said for tailoring.

Marlie was staring but couldn't help it. *He's not your type,* her sense of self-preservation protested weakly as a massive reconfiguring of what Marlie found attractive was underway. It was like reformatting her hard drive and wiping off all the sexy-men-in-jeans files and replacing them with James Bond clone files. Which, Marlie now thought, were not bad files at all.

And then Ty smiled, which was just killer. She didn't even care that he knew it.

"Isn't he handsome?" Axelle asked.

"Yes," Marlie agreed, and sighed, all pride gone.

Still smiling, Ty gave her a mock bow, allowing her to save face and pretend she'd been kidding with the sigh.

Except she hadn't been.

"We upgraded his dinner jacket." Axelle smoothed the already smooth satin lapel and Ty turned his smile her way.

Marlie felt a pang. Sure it felt like good old jealousy that Ty was gaga about Axelle and not her, but it really and truly was only a sign that she was ready for a man in her life again. Like now. Right now.

"You both look stunning," Marlie said, so they'd know she wasn't jealous. "Axelle, you're going to look so beautiful up on the stage. Silver was a good choice."

"Thank you, Marlie." Axelle tore her gaze away from Ty. "I thought pewter was a fresh color for the season."

Okay, it was called pewter instead of silver. Whatever. Marlie was through gushing. They were gorgeous. They knew it. She wished they would leave.

"And thank you for working so hard this afternoon," Axelle said. "I hope we get bidders from the website."

"I do, too." Especially since Marlie had invested in extra webcams so she could show the action as well as close-ups of the items. "I'll be watching and handling everything from here and Randy is going to be sitting right in front with his laptop. We had a dry run a little bit ago." She'd already told Axelle all this, but the woman was a maniac about details. "Everything works great. Now go." She made shooing noises as Ty flashed her another smile.

Her breath caught. He hadn't *meant* to smile at her like that, had he? That sexy, full-of-promise smile? No, that was leftover from the smile he'd given Axelle.

Calm down. But her heart beat hard just the same.

They left, after subjecting Marlie to a touching scene where Ty draped Axelle's wrap around her shoulders. Good thing, since when Axelle turned to go through the door, she appeared to be missing the back of her gown. Marlie wondered if Ty could make it all the way to the auction without ripping the thing off her.

Alone, Marlie felt antsy and restless. This afternoon, when she'd been setting up in the hotel ballroom, Axelle had introduced her to several men and they all seemed very nice. But.

But you don't want 'very nice', you want Ty.

No, she didn't. She wanted a man. Marlie tried visualizing a man. Any man who pushed her buttons. Ty popped into her mind. *Get out of my head,* she thought irritably. The problem was that there weren't any other men in her head. So she studied The Twelve Men of Christmas, flipping through their bios and pictures on the site. They'd revved her engine the other day, but now, not even the drummer, her favorite, was doing anything for her.

She thought of Ty and the warm fuzzy feelings started again.

Not good. So she thought of Ty being irritated, Ty being oblivious, Ty with his stuff all over her house, and the fact Ty had never looked at her the way he looked at other women.

Still warm. And the fuzziness had turned to tingles. What was the matter with her? For years, the only warm feeling she'd had for Ty had been resentment. Certainly nothing had tingled. Even when their moms had suggested he move in with her, all she'd felt was relief. It was Ty and she wouldn't have to deal with the normal man/woman issues.

Well, now she was having issues.

Which was bad, because Ty was not available. Which was good, because there was no way she could fit into a dress like the one Axelle was wearing. Axelle was tall and model thin. Ty's type. Marlie was average and round. Not Ty's type.

But not as round as she'd been. Her jeans snapped at the waist for the first time since he'd moved in, for which she was grateful, since she'd needed to wear them to set up cameras and crawl around trying to find electrical outlets.

Axelle had also worn jeans this afternoon.

Denim looked entirely different on Axelle. Marlie had fit right in with the technical crew and Axelle had fit right in with the socialites. They both wore jeans, a top, and a jacket, but anyone entering the hotel ballroom automatically went straight to Axelle as the person in charge.

Although Marlie was not jealous of her, sometimes she thought she should be. They'd never be best buddies, but they didn't have to be. Axelle was still her client. She'd always been friendly in a professional way, with the extra touches of thoughtfulness that made people want to deal with her and return to her restaurant again and again.

For example, this afternoon, when Marlie had complained about how Houston's humidity had made her hair impossible, Axelle had given her a purse-sized bottle of the defrizzing product she used.

Marlie hadn't cared much about her appearance in the past couple of years. The fact that she'd spent time trying to tame her hair this afternoon was another sign she was ready to reenter the dating scene. She thought of Ty and his we-will-mate-soon smile and shivered.

She wanted a man to look at *her* that way. And the sooner she found one, the sooner she'd stop hoping that man would be Ty.

TYLER WAS ENJOYING HIMSELF way more than he thought he would when Axelle first told him about the auction. She wore a dress that clung to her like liquid silver—where there was a dress to cling. And man, did she have a body for it to cling to. As she worked the crowd in the hotel ballroom, welcoming everyone, making sure the drinks flowed, encouraging people to view the auction items, and doing what she did best, Tyler watched the double takes from the men as she turned her naked back to them and glided to the next group. She was like a glittering ornament, a prize who would enhance the stature of the man who won her.

And he was the one who'd get to take her home. But not to his home. His wasn't finished and Axelle wasn't about to go to Marlie's while Marlie was in it. And technically Axelle didn't have a home, so Ty would be taking her to her brother's home. And departing shortly thereafter.

He was eager to take their relationship to the next level, more eager than Axelle, he suspected. She was a bit of a reach for Ty, and he didn't feel completely solid with her yet, as though there was some test he had to pass. He hoped volunteering to be the auctioneer wasn't the test. But in case it was, he needed to do something else. He should bid on something tonight. He'd already intended to anyway, but now he needed to make a grand, attention-getting, and expensive, gesture. But what would please her? If he was about to drop some major bucks, he'd like to know she appreciated it.

If Axelle were more like Marlie, he could just ask and she'd tell him. Marlie was a completely different type of female, but she had her good points. Ty knew what to expect from her. She was comfortable, dependable, and easy to be around. Restful. He liked that about her, but for the long haul, he wanted some spice and excitement. Not spice and excitement all the time—that would be exhausting—but enough to keep life interesting.

Some guys didn't want any of that. Ty knew men at work who wanted to come home at a certain time and know that dinner was pork chops on Tuesday and Chinese takeout on

Friday, that Sunday afternoons were for kicking back on the couch and watching sports. Marlie was exactly right for those guys. He could see the appeal in that kind of life. Ty, himself, would get bored, but he sure was going to miss living with her. He never had any worries on the domestic front, and in return, he was glad to check out the funny noises in her car or fix a leaky faucet. They'd fallen into the pattern as though they'd been living together for years. Marlie was made to be a wife and mother.

While Ty understood what her ex had been feeling, he bet that someday, Eric would be kicking himself for not realizing how good he'd had it.

Heck, if the timing were different, Ty might be tempted by her, himself. But he wasn't ready for a tame life of domestic responsibility. And when he was—if he ever was—Marlie would probably be married with a couple of kids.

Axelle had stationed Ty by the auction tables to answer questions and distribute brochures. Nobody had any questions and everybody already had a brochure. Nothing much was going on yet. Truthfully, he was getting a little bored. Marlie, home alone, was probably really bored. So, when he spied one of her webcams, he turned away from the room, stuck his head right in front of the lens, and made a silly face.

MARLIE SNORTED CHICKEN noodle soup.

If Axelle caught him doing that, Ty was toast. Marlie had spent all afternoon working with her and knew the woman wanted every detail to be perfect tonight. Not only was this Axelle's first fundraiser, it was also the first fundraiser for the Midtown Mentors. While it was a good program, Axelle had taken on the auction as a vehicle to draw attention to her restaurant. She wanted to impress the type of people who would frequent Ravigote with a classy, perfect-down-to-the-last-detail event. So if she had seen Ty making faces at Marlie, she would have had a cow. But only prime beef, of course.

Marlie laughed, once she'd gotten soup out of her nose. Ty was lucky she hadn't been streaming that particular camera over the internet.

On the other hand, he probably wouldn't have cared. That made her laugh again and she remembered the time she'd sprained her ankle playing soccer when she was eight, and she'd had to go to the camp infirmary. She'd been trying not to cry because her parents hadn't been located yet and Tyler, who was supposed to walk her back to their cabin, wouldn't know where she was. He was mad at her, anyway, because he wanted to go to the swimming pool with his team because of some girl he liked. Marlie was scared until she saw Tyler's head pop up outside the examining room's window. He'd made faces at her from behind the nurse, and she'd tried not to laugh so the nurse wouldn't make him go away.

He'd made that same face just now. He didn't have much of a repertoire. Still, tears pricked her eyelids because Tyler could have gone to the pool that day after all. But instead, he'd stayed with her until her parents came and drove them back to the cabin.

She hadn't thought of the incident at all since then.

Marlie wished she could communicate through the camera. Sure, she had his cell number, but it would have been more fun to make faces back at him.

She punched in his number and watched him straighten and reach for his phone. "You goof! What are you doing?"

"Checking to see if you were paying attention."

She laughed. "Why aren't you mixing and mingling?"

"I have brochure duty." He held them up to the webcam.

Huh. Axelle had stashed him off in the corner? Not a good sign. "Where's Axelle?"

"Oh, around here somewhere." Ty appeared unconcerned

as he drew back from the camera and looked around the room. Marlie saw him go still, an intent look on his face that told her Axelle was nearby.

Marlie switched cameras until she could see Axelle sweeping across the room toward him. He closed his phone and slipped it into his pocket, her call to him forgotten.

AXELLE SWOOPED IN AND snagged Ty's drink, guzzling it down and making a face. "What *is* this?"

"Ginger ale." He'd wanted to stay sharp.

"With *sugar?*" She looked horrified.

As though she needed to worry about her weight. She was perfect. Absolutely perfect. "A little sugar won't hurt you."

"I thought this was scotch and soda." Axelle looked around. "I need alcohol."

There isn't enough alcohol in the world, Ty thought, nonplussed at seeing Axelle nervous. "You'll be fine," he assured her, and then amped it up. "Once you start the auction, all you have to do is throw a few smiles out there and the bids will come rolling in."

"I hope so," she said, taking a deep breath. "There aren't as many guests as I'd hoped."

Ty looked around. "There are lots of people here."

"But most are members who've already donated something for the auction. They won't be as generous when it comes to bidding. I'm just afraid that if the items do not sell for at least what they are worth, people won't be as willing to support us next year. Or even willing to have an auction."

Seeing Axelle as anything other than supremely confident made her more human to Ty and less out of his league. He slipped his arm around her waist to give her a reassuring hug. His hand skimmed across bare skin. He stopped breathing so he could fully savor the feel of his hand on her back. When he became light-headed, he inhaled and asked with all the casualness of which he was capable, "So, this afternoon, did you introduce Marlie to any guys?"

Axelle blinked slowly, as though incredulous at the change in subject. "Several. Although I did not first ask if they were single and looking," she said, sounding snappish.

Ty slowly withdrew his arm. "Who knows if they're her type, anyway? She just needs to get out there."

Axelle gave him a smile he had no idea how to interpret. "Perhaps it is a little early for her to have a type."

Now, that was a definite slam. "Hey. You're not jealous of Marlie, are you?"

Axelle was immediately contrite. "That sounded awful, did it not?" She put her hand on his arm, which warmed and distracted him. "I have butterflies and it is time to start the auction." She squeezed. "Wish me luck."

Ty captured her hand before she could withdraw it, pulled it to his shoulder and kissed her.

He didn't kiss Axelle nearly enough. He was ready to forget the auction and everyone in the ballroom until someone announced that it was time to begin. He became aware of an insistent pushing and Axelle turned her face away.

"Good luck," he whispered.

As she swept through the crowd and climbed the steps to the podium, he admired her back and the way the dress moved and felt good that other men envied him…. Then he realized that she hadn't kissed him back.

DUE TO THE FACT THAT Ty was right in front of the webcam that would be providing close-ups of the auction items when he planted one on Axelle, Marlie got a very good demo of his kissing technique. The way he masterfully drew her toward him, determined and passionate… She sighed deeply. And she zoomed in with the camera, which was weird, because did she really need to know how Ty kissed? Really?

And the look on his face as he watched Axelle waltz away. Marlie's own private movie. All she needed was popcorn.

But there wasn't time for popcorn. The auction was about to begin.

Axelle was introduced and she stepped up to the podium as though she owned it. Marlie centered her in the frame and checked out the other cameras she'd positioned around the room. Axelle was going live over the internet.

"...coming this evening. As you know, the Midtown Business Mentor program provides a positive alternative to less desirable urban influences. Youth aged thirteen to sixteen are mentored by representatives from professions that interest them. They work as junior interns and gain valuable experience and skills they can use in their chosen field. Instead of roaming the streets, they learn software programming, commercial food preparation, first aid, and sales skills. We are here tonight to raise money to purchase a van that we can use to transport students from their schools to the businesses."

Beautiful, competent, and doing good work. No wonder Ty was smitten with her.

Marlie panned the crowd. Not quite as large as Axelle had hoped. Marlie tightened the frame so the empty edges of the ballroom were out of the picture.

She's so hot. Randy, down front with his laptop, messaged her. If she were up for bids, I guarantee you we'd get the van.

Marlie frowned.

Axelle turned to one of the assistants and flashed the side of her bare back.

Smokin'.

I get the picture, Marlie messaged back.

Sorry. Forgot you were a girl.

That's okay, Marlie thought. *So did I.* She looked at the bouquet of flowers Axelle had sent. Only one of the flowers appeared past its prime. There was still a lot of life left in them. And there was still a lot of life left in her, too.

The auction got underway with a couple of spa baskets. Nothing special, just some warm-up items to get the crowd going. Next up was dinner for four at Ravigote, Axelle's restaurant. For this item, her brother joined her at the podium.

He was better looking without the chef's uniform he'd worn in the dating package picture. A lot better looking. He rocked a tux as well as Ty did. And he had a way of sweeping his gaze over the crowd and lingering on the females. Even remotely, Marlie felt its effect. She zoomed in on Paul instead of the certificate on the display table. Paul was going to sell this, not the food or the clip art on a certificate.

Bidding started at an embarrassingly low amount. Marlie had seen the menu prices. Dinner for four with wine could run several hundred dollars easily.

There was an awkward silence when Axelle hesitated before tapping her gavel and announcing that the dinner would go for the bargain price of one-hundred and seventy-five dollars. Paul was gracious, but not overly so.

They'd also donated a romantic dinner for two and Marlie messaged Randy to hold it for later.

She was blogging live on the website and increased her use of exclamation points in relaying the bargain price. She also encouraged everyone to get ready to bid on the dinner for two later.

The energy went out of the auction after that. Rather than moving quickly, Axelle slowed down in hopes of increasing the bidding. Mistake.

Tell her to keep it moving Marlie messaged Randy.

Moments later, an assistant whispered in Axelle's ear and she raced through a series of lower-ticket items. Now that was too fast.

The Wimberley, Texas B&B weekend went for an embarrassing one hundred dollars. But Marlie was getting web interest, *significant* web interest focused on one item: The Twelve Men of Christmas dating package. According to the comments on the blog, nobody wanted to bid on anything else in case they needed money for the package. Marlie asked how many were waiting for The Twelve Men of Christmas and the comments flooded in.

Marlie called Ty's cell, hoping he'd answer.

"What's up?"

"Tell Axelle to take a five-minute break and auction the dating package."

"Now? But that's the big finale."

"Women aren't bidding because they want to have enough money for it. Tell her to auction it now so the losing bidders can buy something else. I've got extreme web interest."

"I don't know. She's got everything planned."

"And how's that working for her?"

Ty didn't answer right away. "Not horrible."

"Her brother was ready to strangle her after dinner at their restaurant went so cheap." Marlie panned the crowd until she saw Ty off to the side, hand over one ear as he spoke to her.

There were no bids on the next lot.

"Ty, I'm telling you, it's time to auction the dates. Use the break to make sure all the women have fresh drinks. Play some peppy music and get the energy going. I'm opening up bidding online."

"Will do."

She heard the click and watched him pocket his phone before striding toward the podium. He looked confident and manly and—

Item picture? Randy messaged.

Oops. She'd been distracted.

But that was okay because Ty had convinced Axelle to

announce a break while the men from the dating package gathered up front to be introduced.

Marlie dutifully blogged a wild excitement about the yummy men, sprinkled a bunch of exclamation points around, and started rumors about the number of buying cartels.

Maybe they weren't rumors, she thought as clusters of women gathered. When the pens came out, Marlie zoomed in and let the online bidders see their competition. Better text your friends, she suggested, and used another camera to focus on the gathering men.

The break was longer than five minutes, because the men were getting props. Marlie could sense the energy in the room building at the anticipation.

The online traffic was hopping, too.

And then it happened—a confirmed online bid. Randy messaged that he'd seen it, too, and Marlie exhaled in relief. At least Axelle's main auction item would make the minimum bid of six hundred dollars. She hoped it would go for ten times that, but Marlie thought she was being optimistic.

Online interest was strong as the men were introduced, with another bid coming in when the adorable drummer in a kilt pretended to show everyone exactly what he was wearing under it.

"As if spending time with a dozen fascinating men is not enough, as a memento, the lucky winner will receive a silver bracelet and a charm after each Twelve Days of Christmas date," Axelle informed the crowd. "I have been asked to say that if a group wins the auction, the auction committee will see that each lady receives a bracelet." A ripple of excited murmuring broke out.

"We have confirmed bids from web bidders, so I am happy to say that I'm looking for six hundred and fifty dollars," Axelle announced.

There was a flurry of bidding and applause broke out when

the amount reached one thousand dollars. There was one more bid online for twelve hundred and then a lot of disappointed posts when five women on the hotel floor bumped it up to fifteen hundred dollars where it stuck.

If you're going to bid, now is the time, Marlie posted. Twelve fun dates for a hundred and twenty-five dollars each? Come on! It's for charity!!!

No response.

Maybe she should have added another exclamation point.

Maybe Axelle should have auctioned them separately. Marlie felt for the guys, but this was not good.

"Two thousand," someone said. A man someone.

Ty.

He was sweet to support Axelle like that, but unless he was prepared to buy the package, he'd better watch it. Marlie wasn't up on auction protocol, but it might be unethical for the auctioneer's boyfriend to drive up the bidding.

Still, Ty's bid started the bidding again. However now, it seemed stuck at twenty-two hundred.

Ty NOTED THE STRAIN ON Axelle's face. He knew what was at stake for her. Axelle wanted entry to the Houston social scene so Ravigote would become a "see and be seen" place. The expense account meals that had been the restaurant's mainstay had dried up, so Axelle hoped to tap into a new customer base—the ladies who lunch and the charity circuit. She had held dinner meetings at the restaurant, and was catering the food at cost tonight. A success would attract attention. A failure would, too.

He saw her gaze dart repeatedly to the side and looked over to see a film crew from the local news. She'd sent out press releases, but it was too bad that the bidding wasn't going well for her centerpiece auction item.

Impulsively, he raised his bidding paddle and called out, "Twenty-five hundred" just to stir things up.

He felt the glare of the video light point his way and kept a smile on his face as he ignored it.

His bid rekindled interest and bidding started up again, but only in twenty-five dollar increments.

"Do I hear three thousand?" Axelle asked, her smile a little too fixed.

"Twenty-five hundred seventy-five."

A group of giggling young women in seriously short black dresses next to Ty went through their purses and called out, "Make that twenty-five ninety-five!"

One of the date group, the Milk Man, pulled a bill out of his wallet and jogged to the women and back to the lineup amid much laughter. The camera crew was trained on the girls as one waved the money over her head. "Twenty-six hundred!"

It would have made a good story for the bidding to end there and Ty could see that the guys in line certainly wanted it to end there, but Axelle looked ready to cry.

The news reporter was interviewing one of the girls. "Why are you bidding on the dates?"

The girl looked at her and then over at the men. "Duh!"

"Yes, that is a bunch of good-looking guys." Unfazed, the reporter held her microphone to another girl. "How about you?"

"It's a great way to meet men," she said. "You get to go out, have a good time, and it's all for charity."

Another girl leaned toward the microphone. "And if you click with somebody, there's nothing in the rules that says you can't keep dating." She giggled.

Yeah. It was too bad Marlie—

Marlie.

Ty remembered Marlie typing captions for the men's photos.

She seemed to like them. All of them, or at least the eight whose pictures he'd seen her work on. Twelve dates. Twelve nights—or days—it didn't matter. What mattered was that a winning bid would get Marlie out of the house on twelve occasions *and* make a grand gesture for Axelle. And might possibly even be a tax write-off. Did it get any better?

"The bid is twenty-six hundred," Axelle gamely cut through the crowd noise. "Do I hear—"

"Three thousand," Ty said, and the crowd hushed. The girls and the reporter looked disappointed. The men looked uncomfortable and the camera light swung Ty's way once more.

"Wait!" called one of the girls. The camera group swung back.

Another group had approached them, apparently combining resources.

"Thirty-five hundred!" the new buying cartel shouted, jumping up and down.

"Four thousand," Ty bid, and smiled at Axelle. She smiled back.

It was going to be worth it.

"Forty-five hundred." He was surprised to hear from the group. They sounded more determined than excited now.

The reporter had been approaching him, but stopped and waited. The camera panned the line of men, some of whom were staring at him and murmuring.

Axelle raised her gavel, obviously about to close the auction.

"Five thousand," Ty called. He smiled at Axelle.

She didn't smile back.

The girls looked at him resentfully and the reporter jogged over to him.

"The bid is five thousand dollars," Axelle said, her accent more pronounced than usual.

There was silence. "Sold to the gentleman in the back who had better have a very good explanation."

The reporter faced the camera. "Alicia Hartson here with the surprising winner of The Twelve Men of Christmas dating auction. What is your name, sir?"

"Tyler Burton."

"You just bought twelve dates with men. And the question everyone wants to know is, why?" She stuck the microphone in his face.

"Not for me." There was laughter, most of it relieved. "The mentors program is a very good cause and I wanted to support it. But even more, I want to express my appreciation to my friend, Marlie, who has put up with me living at her house while mine is being built. She works really hard, and could use a few nights out on the town. And so, Marlie—" he twisted until he was facing one of the webcams "—Merry Christmas!"

5

MARLIE CLASPED HER HANDS over her mouth. Oh, no, he didn't.

But there was Tyler, talking to a reporter, after he'd dropped a bundle at the auction.

For her. Or rather for Axelle, who was basking in the lime-light with him as he stroked her naked back.

Right. "A few nights out on the town." He'd bought that package for himself—to get Marlie out of the house.

What, he didn't trust her to find somebody to date by herself?

Then again, she'd found Eric.

Still. She picked up her cell phone to text him her refusal but stopped. He looked so happy. Axelle looked happy. The dating dudes looked glad to get out of the spotlight. The reporter was getting a twist on the usual charity auction story, so she was happy.

And Marlie was...embarrassed. But twelve men, including the drummer who was bashfully cute. Twelve chances to find someone, someone other than Ty. And these men all had friends they could introduce her to if they didn't personally click with her, so this could be a shortcut to a new relationship.

She could act all offended and refuse, or she could accept the gift and enjoy herself, especially with the drummer, Mr. Milk, and the swan guy. Partridge in a Pear tree wasn't bad, either.

Oooo. Axelle's brother was Three French Hens. Marlie grinned. This was going to be good.

TYLER CAME BACK DOWN TO earth after Axelle's enthusiastic and prolonged thank-you kisses. Part of him was keenly aware that the auction was in a hotel and that there were rooms with beds just a short elevator ride away. But answering Axelle's exuberant gratitude with "Shall I get us a room?" seemed cheesy. And so here he was, back in Marlie's garage, without Axelle. Even worse, he had to face Marlie.

No way had she missed him making the biggest auction bid of the night, so he'd been expecting a call or a text, but his phone had been silent. He had no idea what that meant. Probably nothing good.

Had he hurt her feelings? That hadn't been his intent.

All right, then. Time to go inside and face the music.

The garage door opened into a hallway that led to her office, which he had to pass to go upstairs. He was tempted to sneak by, if he could, but he'd no more turned the key in the deadbolt when Marlie came skipping down the hall and flung her arms around his neck.

"Oh, thank you, Ty! That was such a sweet and generous thing to do!"

Of all the scenarios he'd imagined, a thrilled Marlie was not one of them.

She hugged him tightly and his arms automatically encircled her. She was soft everywhere and there was more of her than there was of Axelle. Not a bad thing, but different. Her ponytail tickled his nose as she turned her head and kissed his cheek. Twice.

He drew her closer. Reflex, he told himself. Her head fit just below his shoulder and his hands fell naturally in the small of her back. She felt so comfortable and she smelled like fabric softener.

Tension left his body. Why had he been tense, anyway?

Resting his chin on the top of her head, he felt as though he'd come home. Well, he had. Her home, at least. Imagine walking in the door to this every night. He could leave the world behind and lose himself in—

Whoa. Marlie could be every bit as seductive as Axelle. For a minute there, she had him seeing hearts and flowers and butterflies as birds chirped in the background.

He raised his head and loosened his hold to find her looking at him questioningly.

"Everything okay?" she asked, pulling back a bit more.

He reluctantly let his arms slip away, disappointed that the world's greatest hug had ended. "I thought you might be a little mad at me."

"Mad?" She did a pretty good fake astonishment. "No, I'm not mad. I was surprised and embarrassed and my first impulse was to refuse to go out with any of them. But then I got to thinking." She turned and he followed her back to her office. "This is dating sink or swim. I'm rusty and what a great way to practice. If I mess up, big deal. Tomorrow is another man."

"Good. Great!" She was taking this awfully well. "Because that's what I was thinking."

Marlie gave him a look. It was the same expression Axelle wore when he told her a little sugar wouldn't hurt her.

"That is not what you were thinking," Marlie said. "You wanted to rescue your girlfriend's auction and impress her, hoping that she would show her gratitude in ways you'd both find mutually enjoyable. And she'd be able to show them here because I would be out dating my way through a Christmas carol."

It was exactly what he'd thought, but summed up much better. Marlie didn't seem upset by it.

She shut down her computer. "Not only that, but it was all for charity. Ty, you are brilliant."

Well, that's kind of what he'd thought, but he knew everyone might not agree. "Thank you. I hope you enjoy yourself."

"That's the plan. You've given me an opportunity and I intend to make the most of it."

This was working out *really* well.

She moved to her printer and removed some papers. "I've got to hurry up and buy a bed."

Ty had a little trouble following the conversation trail and when he did, he didn't like where it was leading. Her first act, when learning she would be going out with a dozen different men, was to buy a bed?

Tyler didn't feel quite so brilliant anymore. "Marlie, be careful. I know it's been a while, but don't...overcompensate." He didn't want her sleeping her way through all twelve verses.

"Overcompensate for what? I've been sleeping on a loveseat for three days."

"Right. But don't buy the first bed you see. Take your time. Check them out. Bounce on the mattress before you sleep on it. Don't get distracted by fluffy pillows and pretty sheets and blankets. Remember that it's what's inside the mattress that counts. Once you buy it, you'll be sleeping on it for years."

"Okay," she said slowly. "I have bought a bed before."

"But it didn't work out, did it?"

She held up the printouts. "That's why I've spent the last three days researching online."

"Online is one thing," Ty told her. "In person is completely different."

"Which is why I'm going bed shopping tomorrow." She looked at him strangely.

"And that's good," he told her. "Because buying a bed is a big decision. And when you make a *big decision,* you should give it a lot of thought before you...decide."

"Are we still talking about beds?"

"They're complicated," Ty said.

They stared at each other. A few beats went by before Marlie changed the subject.

"I got a text from your reporter friend."

"I don't have a reporter friend."

Marlie ignored him. "Alicia Hartson wants to interview me and possibly show up on some of the dates. You're about to become a romantic legend."

Ty grinned. "I don't see a down side to that."

"Maybe not for you, but I don't need to look pitiful and have this turn into a 'Marlie's Quest for Love' series. So heads up, I'm not saying anything about Eric. I may tell stories about you as a little kid, parts of which may even be true."

"Hey!"

"Oh, please. Nobody cares. They just want a good story. You'll come out looking good."

"I'm already looking good," Ty said. "I just spent five grand on your Christmas present."

Marlie gave him a wicked grin. "And I'm just your roomie. I can hardly wait to see what you get for Axelle."

She had a point. "Neither can I."

MARLIE HAD EXPECTED MORE TIME before A Partridge in a Pear Tree called for his date, but the morning after the auction, Jason Fairgood asked her to dinner at the Flaming Pear restaurant. When she hung up the phone, she saw Ty scowling at her from the doorway.

"You told that guy where you live?" he asked.

"He's going to pick me up."

Ty shook his head. "It's a first date. You live in the big city now. You don't go telling a strange guy where you live. You meet him somewhere."

"Jason is not a strange man. He's a mentor and Axelle knows him. In fact, I imagine she screened everybody she auctioned off for dates, even if they'd already been vetted to work with kids. If anything bad happens, there will be horrible publicity."

"Which you'll find comforting in your hospital bed."

He was going to be a stinker about this. "Okay, I get your point. When I'm dating outside the auction men, I'll be more cautious."

"Thank you," Ty said.

Marlie expected him to leave for his jog since he was dressed for it, but he lingered. "Where are you going tonight?"

"The Flaming Pear. They have partridge on the menu."

"That's not very original" was Ty's comment.

He didn't seem very enthusiastic about the dates, considering he was the one who'd bought them for her.

As they spoke, Marlie was checking out the restaurant's website. Lots of cutesie flash which quickly grew old and annoying when she had to wait for a cactus to burn every time she tried to navigate to a different page. Apparently the "pear" referred to a pear cactus. "I'm not complaining," she said. "It's a nice restaurant. Other than lunch at Axelle's, I haven't been to a fancy restaurant since Eric and I broke up." Marlie decided that was the way she'd refer to her onetime engagement. It sounded better than "He dumped me out of the blue right before the wedding invitations went out."

Ty still hadn't left, but he wasn't saying anything. She looked up at him.

"I'm sorry, Marlie." His face was serious.

That was unexpected. "For what?"

"I should have taken you out."

"Why?"

"Well, we're living together."

"But we're not *live* living together."

"No, but it's not unheard of for roommates to socialize." He gave her a lopsided smile.

"You mean, spend time with me on purpose?" She cocked her head at him. "Did your mom call and give you a 'be nice to Marlie' lecture?"

"No." He straightened, looking affronted. "I thought of that on my own. I'm not a kid anymore, Marlie. I did mature."

Oh, she knew. "I'm sorry, but—"

"It's okay." He waved off the rest of her apology, opened the front door, and jogged down the steps.

Ty had been acting very different lately. She had to admit that after years of him ignoring her or wishing she wasn't around, his sudden interest was weird.

But not unwelcome.

Marlie closed her eyes. She was going to miss him when he moved out. Just knowing he was home made her sleep easier at night, even if it was on the loveseat in her office.

If his house had been completed in time and he'd moved out last year, it wouldn't have been so bad. But now she was used to him being there. She'd even told him about Eric, and he'd been nice to her—in his way, but still. And fixing her up with all those guys was a unique way to solve the problem of Marlie meeting men and…

She might as well admit it. Marlie had an extremely inconvenient crush on him. It was the crush she should have had years ago, but never did.

But it was going to stay a crush and she'd outgrow it the same as she would have as an adolescent. All she had to do was find someone to take his place. And she was starting tonight.

Ty had accused her of turning into a hermit. She hadn't been that bad, but she was sure out of touch with trends and styles. Unless an event made headlines, she didn't know about it. And she hadn't watched much TV or seen a movie in months.

What was she going to talk to her partridge date about? Website design? If that's what he was into, then not a problem. Anything else, well, it would be a problem. This was not good. Even she'd be bored if she had to date herself.

Marlie had planned to go looking at beds today, but it was going to take her hours to prepare for her first date, post Eric, because she was really out of practice.

When *was* the last time she'd been on a date with somebody other than Eric? College. Seven years ago? *Seven?* She hadn't been on a first date in seven years and now she was getting ready to go on a dozen of them?

Marlie was hit with a bad case of nerves. What was she going to wear? And what about her *hair?*

She turned off her computer, something she *never* did during waking hours, and headed upstairs to explore the depths of her closet.

Way too much time later, she emerged with three candidates, all purchased for what earlier generations called a trousseau.

First, she eliminated one of her choices because it no longer zipped. Tragic. She'd bought it to wear to a wedding shower her neighbors were giving her back home in California. The shower never happened and Marlie had never worn the dress. While she decided between the other two, she washed her hair and blew it dry for the first time since she'd gone home last Christmas.

It looked less frizzy, but she'd forgotten to use the defrizzer Axelle had given her, so Marlie rewet her hair and tried again. Definitely less frizzy this time, but it lay flat against her head and the ends looked scraggly. Not only that, it was dark to just above her shoulders then grew lighter where the ancient highlights kicked in.

No, no way was she shopping for a bed today. She was going to have to get her hair cut. As a walk-in. At a strange salon. On a Saturday. The only stylist not booked on a Saturday was a bad stylist. But could her hair look worse than it did now? Maybe if color was involved, but surely she could chance a trim. Just an inch or so, until she could get an actual appointment.

"So what do you know about this Jason guy?" Ty asked Axelle. He'd called her after he'd returned from his run.

"Jason who?"

"Jason from the auction," he reminded her impatiently.

"There are two Jasons."

"Partridge in a pear tree Jason."

"Oh, the fireman. He's a member of a local wine club. They meet here once a month."

"And?"

"And what?"

He heard clanking in the background. "Is that all you know? Marlie is going to spend an evening with him!"

"Oh, you're so protective, Tyler. Marlie is a big girl. These tablecloths haven't been replaced from lunch service yet," she said to someone.

Then he heard somebody call out, "Axelle!"

He heard an exasperated sigh. "Our sommelier knows him and he's single, I think."

"You *think* he's single?"

"Tyler, it is a dinner, not a life-long commitment, eh?"

She sounded harried, which actually was good. Saturday was Ravigote's busy day and usually Ty avoided calling her. But it was three o'clock, dinner service hadn't started and lunch had ended at two. Tyler backed off. She was right. It was just dinner. "You sound busy. Have reservations increased since the auction last night?"

"Some," she said vaguely.

She didn't have time to chat. He got the message. But he didn't like it. "I'll let you get back to work," he said. "I'll call you after eleven."

"Oh, Ty, I'm much too tired after last night! I could sleep for a week."

Alone, Ty heard. It wasn't as though he *expected* anything in return for his generosity. He *anticipated*. That was different. It would be bad if he didn't look forward to being alone with her.

Disappointed, he considered the irony of being all alone in the house on a Saturday night while Marlie went out on the town.

TYLER HAD JUST SETTLED himself on the couch with a sandwich and beer to watch a football game when he heard Marlie thumping down the stairs. Her date wasn't due for another twenty minutes, but it sounded as though she was already panicked.

Of course she was. Not only hadn't she been on a date in forever, she hadn't been around humans much at all lately, either. Ty schooled his face and prepared to tell her she looked great. Anybody who had spent as much time getting ready as she had deserved to be told she looked great.

"Ty!" she called from the stairs. "I can't decide what to wear. I want you to give me your opinion. And I need you to be honest."

Oh, right. Like he was going to fall for that. He muted the pre-game chatter. "Just wear the outfit that makes you feel the most comf—"

The air left his lungs. He blinked and then he blinked again.

Short. Tight. Red. Blond. Boobs. The images struck him fast and hard. And not necessarily in that order.

Curves. Skin. Legs. Hair.

Secondary impressions were slower as he began to notice more detail.

Lush curves. Pale skin. Shapely legs.

And blond hair. A gleaming, straight waterfall of streaky blond.

Wide, thick-lashed, bambi-brown eyes stared at him. Shiny, crimson lips moved.

Desire flooded his senses, different than his usual intellectually-controlled desire for tall, thin, sleek brunettes.

His body was now in the driver's seat, hooting and hollering for a blond, curvy Jessica Rabbit.

"Ty?"

"Marlie?" The hooting and hollering stopped.

He stared. He didn't know if she stared back because he wasn't looking at her eyes.

"Yeah." She touched her hair. "It was color day at the beauty school. The instructor was showing how lighter layers around the face gives the impression of blonder hair without lifting the color all over. And then he added darker pieces to contour my face and medium streaks for depth…and I'm babbling. I look stupid, don't I?"

Not. At. All. Ty drew air into his lungs because it had been a while since he'd taken a breath. Spots peppered his vision.

Marlie misinterpreted his hesitation. "I knew it. It's too much. Both the hair and…" She gestured down her body. "I haven't had this dress on since I bought it. It's a little snug, but I thought I could get away with it. I'll change." She whirled around and started up the stairs, the rear view as spectacular as the front. There was no evidence that she spent her days sitting.

"No," Ty managed to get out, but his voice was hoarse. He cleared his throat. "No!"

But she was gone.

He stared at the spot where she'd stood, an homage to Jessica Rabbit.

Marlie.

She…she… He'd had no idea she'd been hiding a body like that. And *how* had she been hiding it? Shapeless sweats, sure, but he'd seen her in sleeveless tops, too.

No wonder he'd enjoyed last night's hug.

And her hair… How could the puff-ball ponytail and the blond goddess locks grow on the same head?

On *Marlie's* head.

Even though it was *Marlie,* desire warmed him and he was too stunned to fight it.

This was not good. It was not cool to lust after his housemate. She was like the appliances. She came with the place.

Whatever she'd done to herself, Ty was certain Axelle had not been involved.

Right, Axelle. *Remember* Axelle. Remember her in the silver dress that left her bronzed back bare.

Ty breathed easier. *Do not think of Marlie's curves or the pillowy mounds above her neckline.* Do not think of her hair waving low over one eye in a way that invited him to brush it back and then, as long as he was in the vicinity, dip down and sample her cherry-red lips.

Ty shook his head and reminded himself that cherry-red lips meant lipstick all over his mouth. He hated that. He didn't care how luscious and pouty they looked or how white her teeth—

"Is this better?" Marlie stepped into view.

Black dress, V-neck, no sleeves. Longer. Looser.

She was still blond, of course, and the neckline was deep

enough to be interesting without giving away the store. Still sexy, but with the volume turned down.

Her fingers plucked nervously at the neckline as she waited for him to say something.

This was going to be tricky. He could throw out a casual, "You look great. I like the hair" and turn back to the TV.

Only he'd been staring at her too long to pull off casual. And she deserved much better.

"You look phenomenal."

"IS THAT GOOD?" MARLIE asked. "Because phenomenal could go either way. And you didn't say anything about the red dress."

Ty's mouth worked. "The red dress was stunning."

"Again, not helpful."

"I was stunned."

When Marlie had seen herself in the mirror, she'd been stunned, as well, but she was still getting over the blondness of her hair. Talk about heavily streaked.

After trying several salons without luck, one had suggested the beauty school. They'd been thrilled to tackle the special challenge of her curly hair, and after the cut went well, she'd been talked into the color.

There had been eight students in the class and they'd each taken a turn, laboriously selecting pieces of hair, painting on goop from the bowl and wrapping the strand in foil. The instructor told her the differences between the students would make her streaks look more natural. Marlie told him natural wasn't working for her. That's why she was there.

Afterward, one side of her head was blonder than the other, so he gave her a choice of toning up one side or lowlighting the other. Marlie was feeling reckless and so here she was with more of her hair streaked than not streaked.

She was not going to think about roots until after Christmas.

After her beauty school adventure, she'd come home and put on the red dress, thinking red was a seasonal color. But while the dress, a bandage-type one that people were still wearing, was meant to fit close to the body, Marlie had more body for it to fit close to than when she'd bought it for her honeymoon.

There was a fine line between eyebrow-raising sexy and slutty. And with the hair, Marlie just couldn't tell. So she'd asked Ty.

Even after she'd given him time to adjust to the hair, Ty's face told her what she needed to know. There was shock, but no awe.

She figured her go-to little black dress would be a safe choice. But she hadn't gone to her LBD in a while and the neckline gapped more than she remembered. Maybe it wasn't so safe anymore because Ty's expression told her he was struggling to find the right words.

The right words were probably "change into jeans" or "Drive to the drugstore and buy a box of brown hair dye."

Well, she had no choice. The Flaming Pear was a nice restaurant, so it was either this dress or the red one.

"Forget it," she told Ty. "I'm going to put on my shoes."

"You look hot," he said quietly.

She fanned her face. "It's all the running up and down the stairs."

"Marlie." His lips curved slowly. "You look *hot*. In this dress, you look icy hot. In the red one, you look smokin' hot."

"Oh." He thought she looked hot. *Smokin'* hot. Nobody had ever told her she looked smokin' hot before. She'd received compliments, sure, but hot hadn't been one. She studied his face to make sure he was serious. "When you didn't say anything, I thought—"

"Yeah." He rubbed the back of his head. "What I was

thinking was 'holy mother of *God*, where has she been hiding that body?'. But I didn't want to scare you."

That, she believed. "You wouldn't have scared me."

"I didn't tell you everything I was thinking." His expression was lightly amused, but his eyes told her he was still thinking those thoughts.

He thought she was hot. He liked the way she looked.

But there was no way he was going to get up from the sofa, kiss her senseless, and carry her up the stairs and ravish her.

No matter how much she wanted him to. But that didn't mean she couldn't enjoy knowing he finally saw her as an attractive woman.

"By the way—the hair." He gave her a double thumbs up. "It officially lands you in babe territory."

Marlie grinned, pleased. "I've never been a babe before."

"You've always been a babe." Ty tossed the remote onto the table, oblivious that his football game had started. "You just haven't been operating in babe mode."

That was generous of him, Marlie thought.

"Which is why you should work up to the red dress," he told her.

Marlie laughed.

"I'm serious," Ty said. "That dress is a babe-in-a-crowd dress. It shouts, 'Attention! Babe entering the room!' That's the dress you wear when you want men to acknowledge your babeness. It's not the dress you wear to dinner on a first date with a stranger."

"He's not a stranger!"

"He's a wino."

"Ty!" Marlie laughed. "He's a member of a *wine* club. He's already selected the wines for each course tonight."

"Wines plural? If either of you drinks more than two glasses, I want you to call me. I will come and get you."

"Yes, Dad." She paused. "Isn't Axelle coming over to-night?"

"No," he said. The doorbell rang, not giving Marlie a chance to ask why. "I'll answer the door," Ty said. "You will put on your shoes and make an entrance."

He was acting like a protective big brother, Marlie thought as she climbed the stairs.

Too bad she couldn't think of him that way.

6

TY TOOK SEVERAL DEEP breaths, just to clear his mind. And because his first impulse was to lock Marlie in her room until her bushy ponytail grew back. The world wasn't ready for a blond Marlie *and* the dresses *and* the body. Maybe the frizzy ponytail and the body. Or baggy clothes and the hair. But all of it together?

He heard a knock and headed downstairs. *All right, let's check this guy out,* Ty thought as he opened the door. If he sensed one wonky vibe, the fireman was toast.

A shorter, but more muscular version of himself took one look at Ty's face and stepped back to check the house number.

Ty relaxed his expression. "Are you Jason?" Of course he was Jason. *I'd like to see the partridge in his pear tree,* Marlie had said.

Well, Tyler was here to make sure that didn't happen.

Jason smiled. Ty recognized the smile immediately. It was the patented, "Your daughter is safe with me, sir" smile, perfected by certain young men. Ty had once been one of those young men. He was not fooled by the smile.

"Yes, I'm Jason Fairgood, here for Marlie Waters."

The guy had dimples and knew how to use them. Ty hoped

Marlie was smarter than to fall for a set of dimples, but who knew what condition her brain was in after all that bleach.

They shook hands as Ty said, "Tyler Burton, Marlie's roommate." He held the door open.

"You're the guy who bought our dating package." Jason hesitated. "Okay, man to man—she's a bow wow, right?"

Tyler almost wished he'd told Marlie to wear the red dress. "Depends on your type."

"Ah. Great personality. Say no more."

"Actually, I will say more." Ty stepped into Jason Fairgood's personal space. "You will show her a good time and you will be respectful, got it? Because if I hear otherwise, I will make sure everyone else hears otherwise, too, starting with the reporter who interviewed me last night."

"Ty? Are you threatening my date?" Marlie stood at the top of the stairs, flashing a lot of leg before slowly picking her way down the steps. She wore a pair of killer black sandals with little straps and really high heels. Her toenails were red.

Well, he *had* told her to make an entrance.

Tyler was mesmerized by the pale feet and the straps and the red toes and imagined a woman wearing the shoes and nothing else in bed.

"Noooo problem on showing her a good time," Jason murmured and Ty knew he was thinking the same thing. Only, in this case, the woman was Marlie.

"When I said 'good', I meant 'cordial' and 'pleasant'," Ty stressed.

"I can do better than that," Jason said.

Ty did not want him doing better than that.

When Marlie safely made it all the way to the bottom of the stairs and they were all breathing somewhat normally again, Jason stepped forward, showing his dimples. "Hi. I'm Jason."

"Marlie." She twinkled up at him. When had she ever

twinkled? Ty had never seen her twinkle. Maybe it was the hair.

"We're going to have a *great* time," Jason said, with enthusiastic sincerity and a slightly dazed expression.

What happened to cordial and pleasant? Tyler was relieved Marlie wasn't wearing the red dress. He might have to hide the red dress.

"Oh, I nearly forgot. I've got something for you." Jason pulled a long narrow box from the inside pocket of his sports coat.

"Thank you." Marlie looked thrilled. Inside the box was a charm bracelet, which Ty knew only because Marlie exclaimed, "The charm bracelet!" She held it up and examined the single charm already attached.

"It's a pear," Jason told her. "For Partridge in a Pear Tree. Giving a charm for each date was my idea—well, my sister's idea, but everyone went for it."

"Oh, that's so sweet!" Marlie said, while Ty thought, *lame and corny.*

"Ty, did you see?" She dangled it in front of him.

"Very cute. Shall I—" help you put it on, was what he was going to say, but another man's fingers beat him to it.

Ty watched Jason stand close and fasten the bracelet around Marlie's wrist. Their heads were nearly touching.

Tyler scowled.

Jason and Marlie smiled at each other.

Tyler scowled even more. "Have a *pleasant* evening you two," he said, hating the way he sounded.

"We will," Marlie said with a look over her shoulder that unnerved him. "Don't wait up."

"WHAT'S THE DEAL with you and the guy you live with?" Jason asked after they'd ordered.

Actually Jason had ordered, or rather strongly suggested,

the dishes that would work best with the wines he'd selected. Marlie didn't mind. She didn't know that much about wines and this was a good opportunity to learn.

"Our parents are friends," she answered. "And we saw each other a lot growing up."

"And you never...?" He raised his brows.

Marlie shook her head. "He's only renting a room from me until his house is finished."

"Oh, okay. 'Cause I thought I sensed a little something going on there."

Maybe her wishful thinking. "No," Marlie said. "I'm free and clear."

Jason leaned forward and gave her a sleepy-eyed look. "Now, why is that?"

I'd forgotten about flirting. Marlie leaned forward, too, and watched Jason's sleepy eyes dip to her neckline. "Broken engagement. Buried myself in work."

"Well, tonight, you're going to eat, drink, and be Marlie!" He grinned. "Did you catch what I did there?"

"Yes. When is the wine coming?" Marlie asked, thinking he might have sounded funnier if she'd already had a glass.

"Right now."

And, indeed, a waiter was bringing out an ice bucket.

Good timing, Marlie thought, wondering when Jason was going to live up to the promise of his picture.

Jason waved the wine steward away. "I asked for the wine to be chilled to the proper temperature. We don't want it blooming too quickly."

Marlie didn't know wine bloomed.

Another server brought a plate of pâté and a bread tray from which Marlie was to choose. She indicated an herbed bread, but Jason shook his head. "She doesn't want that one."

"Yes, she does," Marlie said.

"It'll interfere with the wine. We'll have unsalted crackers."

Marlie sniffed the tantalizing scent of rosemary and garlic as the bread basket was whisked away. "The wine had better be worth it, because that bread was still warm."

Jason poured himself a tiny bit of wine. "That's so refreshing that you eat bread." He stuck his nose into his glass.

"Warm and crusty herb bread is worth eating." Marlie watched the retreating waiter because she didn't want to watch Jason. "Unsalted crackers, not so much."

Jason took a sip and held it in his mouth before swallowing. "With a wine this playful, you'll forget all about the bread."

There was something off about that sentence, but Jason was now filling her glass and she didn't want to distract him by asking what he meant. Gratefully, she took a large sip.

"No!"

Marlie jumped and splashed her hand.

"You don't chug it!" Jason lowered his voice. "You savor it."

"I was savoring it. I savor quickly." Marlie dabbed at her hand.

"But you must roll the wine over your tongue so that the sweet, salty, and bitter taste sensors have time to detect the flavors. And then you experience the finish. So many people crowd the finish because they're already drinking again."

Marlie stared at the half-glass remaining of her slightly sour white wine. She was ready to experience a finish right now and it wasn't the wine's. She dutifully sampled the wine as instructed—still slightly sour—and told herself to give the date more than thirty minutes before writing Jason off. She was rusty and he was making an effort and giving up his time and money for charity. She needed to hold up her end. "So you're a fireman."

"It's a good thing, too. If you were any hotter, you'd burst into flames." Jason smiled slowly, allowing his dimples to crease.

Seriously? Marlie polished off the rest of her glass of wine. "I think it's too early for that line."

Jason straightened, shaking his head. "I knew I should have gone with the 'you're smokin'' one."

Marlie laughed. She'd been called smokin' twice in one night. How amazing was that? Jason laughed, too, and after that, she began to enjoy herself. Earlier, he'd come off as arrogantly controlling, but once Marlie relaxed, she realized how much planning and care he'd put into the food and wine pairings, even consulting the chef about the seasonings used in the dishes.

"The guys at the station give me a lot of grief over my hobby," he told her. "I guess I go into lecture mode." And he smiled so charmingly that Marlie didn't mind hearing about grapes and soil and weather and regions and vintages and the cork versus screw top controversy.

Then there was the way he looked at her. Interested. Focused. Attracted. She'd wanted a man to look at her exactly like that and now Jason was doing it. She was flattered and self-aware and caught herself making little gestures and watching as his eyes followed her movements like a cat does before it pounces.

But, much as she enjoyed herself, Marlie didn't want to be pounced on by Jason. Nor was she inclined to do any pouncing herself. Pity. He was certainly good looking.

He's no Ty, came the thought. However, Marlie had anticipated the thought and was able to squash it, mainly because the restaurant lights suddenly dimmed.

A violinist playing "The Twelve Days of Christmas" led a parade consisting of two chefs, two waiters, and the wine steward bearing a platter which they set in the middle of the table.

Marlie stared at a brown pyramid with rosemary twigs stuck in it. And…a bird stared back at her. "Partridge in a Pear Tree?" she guessed, mainly because the violinist had finished and everyone in the entire restaurant was staring at her, waiting for her to say something.

"Yes!" Jason grinned. The chefs beamed. The violinist played a flourish. The other diners applauded. Cameras flashed.

A bright beam of light made her blink as a disembodied voice said, "Alicia Hartson here with Marlie Waters as she begins her Twelve Dates of Christmas with a Partridge in a Pear Tree. Marlie, what do you think of your dinner?"

She hadn't tasted it yet, but talk about a rhetorical question. "It…looks phenomenal." The microphone was still in her face. "The bird head is so life-like. Just stunning."

"Standing with me are the two chefs responsible for this special holiday creation." Alicia turned to interview them. The cameraman went in for a close up of the platter, blocking Marlie's view of Jason.

"We roasted pears and used rosemary for the branches," she heard.

The tree was cute. Cranberries looked like ornaments among the branches. Very clever. Little swirls of lemon and orange peel dangled from the rosemary. And then, of course, there was the bird staring at her.

"Take a look at the partridge." Alicia gestured to the cameraman. "Can we get a close-up? Is the head and tail edible?"

"Of course," one of the chefs replied. "We used jicama, carrots, and beet juice. Then we attached the head and tail to the roasted partridge breast."

An actual partridge? She was going to eat partridge?

Alicia went over to Jason's side of the table as the waiters dismantled the tree and served two plates. "Jason, this is spectacular. The rest of the men making up the twelve dates are going to find you a tough act to follow."

Jason flashed the dimples at her. "I'm always a tough act to follow."

Alicia gave a professionally-amused laugh and turned to Marlie. "So how does it taste, Marlie?"

Marlie stared down at her plate, brilliantly lit by the camera's glare. The waiters had made a nest of rosemary and sliced pear and settled the partridge in it. Jason's plate just had the breast part. "It's too pretty to eat!" She smiled, hoping they wouldn't make her eat on camera.

But no.

"Here, let me." One of the chefs moved forward and decapitated Marlie's partridge.

She flinched. There was a short silence.

"Jason, tell me, will there be a second date?" Alicia asked, diverting attention from the carnage. The camera swung away.

"Well…" Jason stalled and looked Marlie's way.

The chef hovered. "I've got it," Marlie said when it appeared as though he was going to cut a bite and feed her himself.

She quickly cut a sliver of meat, irritated that Jason hadn't answered Alicia. Come on. It wasn't a real question. They were acting here. The mentor program would get a plug, the restaurant would get a plug, and Marlie was going to say that the food was the best she'd ever eaten no matter what it actually tasted like. All Jason had to do was express interest in a second date. It made for a feel-good news story.

She hoped this wasn't being broadcast live. She hoped Alicia would edit out the decapitation and Jason's lingering hesitation. But that meant they had to fill the gap with Marlie's reaction to the food.

She popped the bite into her mouth, determined to give

them plenty of footage. "Mmm." Good thing it actually tasted decent. Cold, but good. She nodded, swallowed, and said, "It's fabulous. The meat is nice and juicy. Sooo good." She cut more, this time with a little bit of pear, put it in her mouth and closed her eyes. "Mmm." She dropped her head back, and, because she still felt the heat of the camera light, added a few more "mmms" as she chewed, exaggerating the movements of her mouth.

"Definitely a second date," Jason said.

TYLER STARED OPEN-MOUTHED AS Marlie faked an orgasm on the ten o'clock news.

Clearly, she missed the whole message behind his bed-buying advice.

Fascinated—and due to the way the camera lingered, he knew he wasn't the only one—he watched her throw back her head and scrunch her shoulders, her eyes closed, her mouth moving in ecstasy as breathy little moans came through his seven-speaker surround-sound audio system. Her newly blond hair glowed in the light and her cheeks were flushed. She wasn't his bland, expressionless, colorless Marlie, but porn-star Marlie. His blood ran hot and cold. Hot, because, well, because. Cold, because Tyler saw Jason's enthralled face in the background. Cold because every straight male with a pulse watching would be trying to find her phone number. And since Marlie's performance was being broadcast right after the football game ended, Ty figured her phone would be ringing all day tomorrow.

And then there were the eleven other men he'd set her up with. Were any of them seeing her performance? If so, they'd get the wrong idea about Marlie. She wasn't like that. Or she hadn't been. Because Tyler knew for a fact that if she had been, her ex would not be her ex.

What had he done? This was his fault. All he'd been trying

to do was nudge her out of her rut and she'd gone all nympho on him.

She had no idea how she looked. That reporter, Alicia, had set her up. Jason had plied her with wine. Yeah. Her cheeks were pink and now she was talking, sounding nothing like herself. The last frame of the story was Jason looking at her, an anticipatory smile on his face.

Ty stared at the TV several moments after the segment ended. Marlie was in over her head and didn't know it. She hadn't dated since college and Jason was no college kid. She was the good-girl wife and mom type, but she was sending out party-girl signals. And she was sending them out on television in a major metropolitan area.

Ty needed to talk with her about those signals. She was a big girl now, but she was still Marlie and he felt responsible. The trick was getting his point across without making her defensive or crushing her new self-confidence.

Ty was watching the weather before he realized that the local news had been postponed until after the playoff game had ended. It was now nearly eleven-thirty and Marlie had been filmed eating dinner hours ago. *Where* was she?

He pictured Jason's expression as the guy watched Marlie giving out the mother of all signals. And that's all he'd see— the sexy blonde with the hot body. He didn't know about the fresh-faced, ponytailed girl inside.

But Ty did, and Jason had better keep his partridge in the pear tree.

Marlie had her cell phone with her, didn't she? Tyler tried to remember if she'd even taken a purse, but he'd been staring at her red-tipped toes and the tiny straps binding her feet and feeling slightly turned on and wondering if it meant he had latent S&M tendencies, then hearing Jason's breathing change beside him and wondering if *he* had S&M tendencies, latent or otherwise. And so no, Tyler hadn't noticed her purse.

Ty clicked off the television and sat in silence. Her sex life was none of his business. Okay, it was a little of his business, since he'd put her in the situation. Enough to justify a casual call—no, a text. A quick text of the "Hey, are you coming home tonight?" variety. Roomie to roomie.

Don't wait up, she'd said.

Ty felt queasy and was angry at himself. They weren't kids any more and his parents weren't going to yell at him if he let Marlie get hurt. He was no longer responsible for her. That had been the pattern of their relationship for so long that it was understandable for him to still feel responsible. Except he'd been living with her for months without feeling the slightest bit concerned about what she was doing or who she was doing it with.

So, why now?

Ty flashed to Marlie in the red dress, Marlie in his arms, and Marlie moaning in ecstasy on television. It would be easy to blame her new hotness.

But it was more than that.

Ty got up from the couch and walked over to the kitchen bar. He picked up the colorful, misshapen ceramic dish where he'd been dropping his keys and change. His mom had sent it when he'd moved in here. Tyler flipped the dish over and read the faded-blue, painted words To Tyler, love Marlie. She'd made it for him after she'd sprained her ankle at camp and had to go to the craft center instead of soccer practice. He'd been horrified at the "love Marlie" part until he saw that she'd made dishes for their parents and friends and signed them the same way. She'd spent three entire days in the craft center. She'd painted a lot of mugs and dishes.

Tyler gently set the dish back on the bar, but continued to stare at it. He cared about her getting hurt because some-how, in the midst of all his resentment that their parents had dumped her on him, they'd become friends.

And as a friend, he was entitled to send a quick text to touch base with her.

Tyler spent the next several minutes trying to strike the right tone and then second guessing whether he should be striking any tone at all.

And then he remembered that she didn't even have a bed to come home to. Oh, this was bad.

He was in the middle of texting when he heard faint voices.

Quickly closing his phone, he turned the TV back on. *Act casual* he told himself as his ears strained for the sound of the door opening and Marlie coming up the stairs. He was pretty sure she wouldn't be inviting the wino fireman inside, considering she didn't have a bed. If they'd wanted a bed, they would have gone to his place. Ty refused to consider that they might have *already* gone to his place.

At last he heard the door close and a groan.

Ty's blood froze and he leapt from the couch. If Jason had hurt Marlie—he stopped at the top of the stairs. Marlie held out one hand to balance herself against the door as she worked off her shoes.

From his vantage point, Ty could see straight down her dress as she bent over. She wore a black bra that did its job and didn't reveal much more than a bathing suit top would have, but Marlie's skin was pale and her curves made interesting shadows that interested him quite a lot.

"Ah." She stood for a moment and wiggled her toes on the cool tile floor. Then she picked up her shoes and started up the stairs inhaling sharply when she saw him.

"Ty! You scared me. Why didn't you say something?"

"I—" *was looking down your dress.*

"Did you wait up for me?" she asked, amused.

Amused? After he'd worried about her? "No. I was watching TV." Marlie reached the top of the stairs and walked past him. He noticed something green stuck in her hair. "There was a really interesting, uh…" He glanced at the TV about the same time Marlie did.

"A shopping channel?"

Even worse, two women were selling mineral makeup.

"Doing some Christmas shopping?" Marlie grinned at him, not fooled.

Ty walked over to the coffee table and grabbed the remote, clicking off the TV. "Always looking for ideas. So how was the date? I saw you on the news." He hadn't meant to add that last part.

Marlie lit up. "It was wonderful," she said, all bubbly. "We ate partridge in a pear tree." She pulled the green out of her hair. "The tree was made out of rosemary and roasted pears. It was really good."

"You looked like you were enjoying it."

She set the twig of rosemary on the counter. "And we had wine." She giggled. "Lots and lots of wine."

"Did Jason have lots and lots of wine, too?" Ty asked carefully.

"Oh, yes. He knows all about wine. And he likes to talk about it, so at first, I didn't think things were going to go well, but he kind of grew on me." She smiled and Ty felt something cold and hard form in his stomach.

"So the more wine you drank, the better he seemed."

She giggled again and swayed. "Oh, yes."

"Dinner was over a long time ago," Ty added.

"We stayed late."

"So you've been at the restaurant all this time?"

"Oh, no." She shook her head and grabbed the banister for balance.

"You're drunk!"

"Nah, just a little buzzed. I'm out of practice."

"Out of practice standing?"

"Oh, Ty. You're so cute." She gave him a flirtatious grin that made him nervous.

"Tell me your date didn't drive you around in that condition!"

"He was in good condition. *Verrry* good condition," Marlie told him, drawing out the Rs.

That's what Tyler was afraid of.

"And I haven't had anything to drink for a couple of hours. I'm just floaty and happy and—"

"*Where* have you been?"

Marlie blinked at his tone. Yeah, he was overdoing it. "The fire station. We walked." She held up her shoes. "My feet hurt."

"Oh."

"Jason wasn't ready to drive."

Ty breathed easier. "That's very responsible of him."

"And I wanted to slide down the pole."

A vision of Marlie and a pole flashed through his mind. Ty gritted his teeth as inevitably he imagined Marlie sliding down the pole into the waiting arms of a large group of fireman. Fresh from their calendar shoot. And they'd been watching the local news and Marlie's enthusiasm about the food. And now they were enthusiastic about Marlie—

"But the station was only one story, so they didn't have a pole." She pouted, sticking out her lower lip.

Do not look at her lip. Do not think about her lip.

Marlie brightened. "They showed me all around and I got to hang out in their kitchen until they got a call. So then it was just Jason and me."

Ty swallowed. *Do not ask.*

"I had a great time." She smiled at him, and then stood on tiptoe and planted a great big kiss on his cheek. "Thank you!" Humming "The Twelve Days of Christmas," she hurried up the stairs.

"Marlie?" he called after her, still feeling the imprint of her kiss on his cheek.

"What?"

Why had he called her back? "I— I'll make up the couch for you. It'll be more comfortable than your loveseat." He should have offered it to her before now.

Her head appeared at the top of the stairs. "You're a sweetie! Hang on and I'll get some sheets."

He walked to the side of the stairs and looked up. Moments later, sheets, a blanket and pillow rained down on him. "Thanks!" he heard her say.

He made up the couch for Marlie, relieved that she was sleeping here instead of with Jason.

Why was he relieved when it wasn't any of his business? He remembered her face with her eyes closed in ecstasy. Yes. That's why he was relieved. Jason hadn't earned that expression. Food, no matter how good, didn't deserve that expression. And if Marlie thought it did, then the day her ex walked out was the luckiest day of her life because *he* sure hadn't been putting that expression on her face.

I could put that expression on her face.

Ty stared down at the couch as he explored the dangerous, but tantalizing thought, liking the idea better and better. Then the rational part of his brain, the part that had been stunned into a coma since he'd first seen Marlie this evening, woke up.

This is not about Marlie, it's about your ego, it told him. *You think Marlie has never had good sex, so you'll show her what good sex is. Then what? Is Marlie supposed to go around sleeping with other men and comparing them to you? Is he as good as Ty? Not as good as Ty? You don't think she'll find anyone as good as you. You* hope *she doesn't find anyone as good as you.*

Wow. He was a real friend, all right.

Marlie came down the stairs wearing her familiar Marlie outfit—stretchy pants and tank top, but without the hoodie.

"Thanks, Ty!" Her hair blond and loose, she flashed him a smile and strode into the kitchen where she got a glass of water.

He'd never seen her walk like that before, confident and self-assured. She usually moused around without him being aware of her.

No one would ever be unaware of *this* Marlie.

Tyler was aware. Very aware. And he was just going to have to get over it. No, not get over it, but acknowledge that his friend was a certified hottie.

Then learn to live with it and her.

7

"WHERE IS MARLIE GOING FOR her turtle dove date?" Axelle asked Ty the next afternoon.

"Somewhere outside," he answered. "Her date showed up with actual turtle doves in a cage. Marlie is supposed to name them and they'll be tagged and released in a bird sanctuary."

Marlie had gone shopping for new jeans for the occasion, barely making it back in time for her date. While she changed, Ty chatted with the bespectacled Tim, who gave off an intellectual vibe. Ty wasn't fooled. It was the quiet ones you had to watch out for.

"Very clever and sweet, but is that the whole date?" As she spoke, Axelle thumbed a number into her cell phone.

"I heard him say something about a picnic." But Tim had said it while watching Marlie walk to his car. Even Ty watched Marlie walk to the car. Those jeans she'd bought had been worth every penny.

"A picnic. What fun." Axelle used a tone that told Ty he'd better never try a picnic with *her*.

Fine with him. He wasn't the picnic type, either.

Ty had been disappointed when the turtle dove guy had called and wanted to see Marlie that very afternoon. There was no way Axelle could get away from the restaurant so, basically, Ty had lost two opportunities to be alone with her.

Right now, they were sitting in Ravigote's bar. It was the two hour gap between the end of Sunday brunch and the beginning of dinner service. Axelle was going over the reservations and calling waitstaff and busboys. Ty was drinking a glass of iced tea and watching her, and trying not to resent her not sparing thirty minutes to focus on him.

He knew she wouldn't come to his office and expect him to drop everything and go play. This was no different. But it felt different. It was Sunday. Nobody was around.

Ty glanced up and down the granite bar. What would happen if he was totally and spontaneously overcome by passion and kissed her boneless before laying her out on the counter and having his way with her?

He looked at her dark head, bent over the schedule as she called the workers. He should at least wait to be spontaneously lustful until she was off the phone.

Axelle, still talking, slipped off the bar stool. Mouthing, "I'll be back," to Ty, she walked into the main dining room.

So much for spontaneity. Ty watched her go and had the disloyal thought that he'd enjoyed watching Marlie walk around the house in her jeans more than he enjoyed seeing Axelle glide around the restaurant in her tight, black skirt.

The thing was, he liked Axelle's black skirts and the way she looked in them. It was what she always wore at Ravigote. And until a couple of hours ago, he would have picked Axelle in the skirt over jeans any time.

Ty stared at the bottom of his iced tea glass. This wasn't working. He drank the rest of the tea, set his glass behind the counter and went to find her. She was at the hostess' desk. He caught her attention, waved goodbye and left.

At least they'd have tomorrow night together. The restaurant was closed on Mondays and that's when Axelle's brother planned to cook for Marlie for her Three French Hens date.

And that's when Ty planned to be alone with Axelle. At last.

IT WAS JUST AFTER DARK when Marlie climbed the stairs to find Ty alone, eating fast food in front of the TV. This time, a football game was playing, so Marlie knew he hadn't been freaking out about her being late, not that seven o'clock was late, even if it was after dark.

He hadn't heard her come in. She smiled as she remembered how adorable he'd been last night, quizzing her date and waiting up for her. He'd done the same this afternoon. He'd been looking out for her and nobody was making him do it. Also, he thought she looked good and it flustered him. Marlie liked seeing Ty flustered for once. And she liked being the one doing the flustering.

Her smile faded as she watched him eat. She was going to have to find someone else to fluster. Mr. Turtle Dove was very nice, but a little low-key for her. He probably wasn't capable of being flustered, although she'd caught him staring at her intently a couple of times. And it wasn't that she was *bored* wandering through the bird sanctuary, but it wasn't her thing. As for the picnic, she knew it would be hard to compete with last night's feast, but sandwiches and cheap champagne didn't even come close. The brownies were good, though. And her legs tingled pleasantly after the walk. Not a bad date, but not a memorable one. She was surprised when he'd asked if she'd go out with him again. She started to decline, but instead asked him to call her after she'd finished her dates. She doubted he would.

Marlie stepped into the room. Ty caught the movement out of the corner of his eye and turned his head. When he saw her, he smiled, looking genuinely pleased to see her.

Marlie stopped. Stopped walking and stopped breathing. Had Ty *ever* looked pleased to see her? Not that she remembered. She took a breath as warmth flooded her. *Don't get used to it. He's leaving.*

"Hey, how was the date?" He muted the game and twisted toward her.

Giving her his attention.

Over football.

And not just any football—the playoffs.

Marlie forced herself to keep it casual, irritated that she was so affected. For years and years and *years,* Ty had looked at her with grim acceptance.

Get a grip. You were both kids. All this means is that you're now adults. "The date was fine," she said, and joined him on the couch. "He was maybe a little too much the crunchy granola, intellectual, rimless glasses type for me, though."

"So what did you name the doves?" Ty ate a French fry and tilted the bag toward her.

"Lovey and Dovey," she said with a straight face and took a fry.

"Because, really, what else can you name them?"

Marlie laughed. "And the dove release was such a non event. The director of the sanctuary was there and gave this little speech because, apparently, these were actual English Turtle Doves. I think they were still jet-lagged because they flew about ten feet into the air and landed on the nearest branch and would not leave."

"Seriously?" Ty grinned.

"Yeah. And Alicia Hartson was there to tape it, so I want to see if it makes the news."

"The news again." Ty stared at the bag of fries. "I didn't realize the dates would be such a big deal. Are you okay with that?"

"Sure." She stole another of his fries. "The more publicity, the more money the auction will raise next year."

"True, but if the attention gets to be a pain, tell me and I'll fix it."

"Fix it?" Marlie laughed. "You mean mob boss fix it?"

"No." He nudged her with his elbow. "I mean phone call fix it."

He would, too, she knew. She could make the same phone call, but it was a nice offer. "Thanks."

Ty turned back to his game. Marlie ate one more fry and then leaned forward to wipe her fingers with the napkins on the coffee table. "I want to put my turtle dove charm on the bracelet before I lose it." She tried using her fingernail to wedge open the silver ring.

She felt Ty's gaze on her before his feet moved from the table to the floor. "Hang on." He went to the kitchen junk drawer and brought back a pair of needle-nosed pliers. Holding out his hand he said, "I'll do it."

Marlie elected not to point out that she was capable of using pliers and let him have his manly moment. She dropped the charm in his palm.

Ty studied the silver birds. "Are you sure those aren't ducks?"

"I don't see any little duck feet."

Ty opened the ring and gestured for her to hold out her wrist. "I'm talking about their schnozzes."

Marlie laughed. "Nobody says schnozzes anymore."

Ty's lips curved. "I just did." He took her hand and propped it on his knee as he fastened the charm to the bracelet.

My hand is on his knee. Try to breathe normally.

As he worked with the tiny charm, his fingers brushed her wrist sending tingles up her arm. She could feel her heart pick up speed.

She had not experienced a single solitary tingle this entire afternoon. There had been a couple of tingles last night, but that might have been because her feet had gone to sleep in the strappy shoes.

Ty wasn't even trying to flirt or anything and here she was, tingling, while he was totally oblivious and taking *forever* to get the charm attached.

"There," he said at last and released her hand. He glanced up as she all but jerked it away from his knee. Their gazes collided and held for about half a second longer than normal.

He knows about the tingling. Maybe not the tingling specifically, but he sensed that something was going on with her.

How embarrassing. It was okay to think he was good looking, but it was not okay to lust after him and waste all the dates. There was plenty of lust-worthy material ahead and she should forget about Ty and start taking advantage of her Christmas present—beginning with Axelle's brother tomorrow night.

"I'VE JUST HAD THE MOST marvelous idea," Axelle had said when Ty had called her that morning. "You can bring Marlie to the restaurant tonight and we'll all eat in the kitchen together!"

It was not a marvelous idea, which he'd made the mistake of saying. Axelle had become very huffy, and so Tyler found himself driving Marlie to the restaurant.

Where he would *not* be alone with Axelle.

And that was not the worst of it. No, the worst of it was that Marlie was sitting right next to him and she was wearing the red dress.

The. Red. Dress.

The one that clung to her.

The one that made it difficult to maintain eye contact with her.

The one that made him breathe shallowly.

"The black dress seemed stuffy for eating in a kitchen," she'd said. "Red is so much more festive."

Festive is what she called it? She was a party all by herself in that dress.

She was doing this on purpose. He'd admitted that he thought she was pretty hot, and now she was using it against him. Ty forced himself to stare straight ahead as he drove, but his peripheral vision was sharper than it had ever been.

The evening was headed for disaster, that's all there was to it. Axelle and Marlie were two completely different types and somehow, Ty knew that was going to be bad. He was on edge and bubbly, bouncy Marlie was not helping.

"Paul said he'd invented a chicken trio dish just for tonight. If it's really good, he'll put it on the menu as Poulet Marlene. Isn't that cool?"

"Very cool." *If you're into having chicken named after you.*

"I like the way Paul says my name—Mar*lain*. It sounds so sophisticated. And poulet is a sexy word. Don't you think?"

"Chicken?"

"Poooolay."

Ty glanced at her as he turned into the restaurant parking lot.

"Poooolay," she said again, her lips forming a pouty kiss. "Is sexy, no?" Her accent sounded horrifyingly like Axelle's.

"If you think a word that starts with 'poo' is sexy."

"Tyler!" She gave his arm a mock slap as she laughed.

He parked the car and got out, inhaling the cool night air. Oh, she had all the flirting moves down pat. He didn't know if she was a quick learner or if it had come naturally.

Didn't matter, really.

Okay. He was going to do this. He didn't know if Axelle was avoiding being alone with him or protecting her brother from

Marlie after seeing her on the news the other night, but Ty was going to proceed as though everything was delightful.

He opened the door for Marlie and watched as she wiggled her way out of the car, her dress riding up and her top riding down.

Oh, everything was just peachy keen.

"Woops!" She smiled and unselfconsciously tugged up her neckline and shimmied her dress down her thighs.

A great calm descended upon Ty, the calm of the doomed man.

At least he had Paul's reaction to look forward to.

Marlie was to come to the kitchen entrance at the back of the restaurant. Ty knocked, expecting Axelle to answer, but the chef, himself, opened the door.

His eyes widened in appreciation. "Marlene!"

He did say it like Marlaine, Ty noticed as Paul took both Marlie's hands in his. Pulling them wide, he gave her a thorough once over.

"Look at you. You are *ravissant!*" Drawing her hands together, he bent and kissed them.

Way over the top. Ty tried to catch Marlie's eye, but she was blushing and simpering and generally eating this up with a spoon.

Ty rolled his eyes, but no one was paying any attention to him.

At that moment, Axelle entered the kitchen, her gaze fixed on Marlie and her brother. "So good of you to come," she said, sounding much less enthusiastic than she had when she'd suggested they all eat together tonight.

"I've been looking forward to it." Marlie still held Paul's hands.

He bent his head and lowered his voice. "I trust I won't disappoint."

"Oh, no," Marlie assured him. "You could never disappoint me."

Axelle's gaze darted back and forth between her brother and Marlie.

It did not dart toward him, so Ty went to stand by her. She aimed a distracted kiss in the general area of his cheek. "Marlie has really...bloomed, hasn't she?"

"She certainly has," Ty said, and drew a sharp look from Axelle. "In a stacked blonde kind of way," he added.

"Some men like that, I suppose," Axelle said.

Just the ones with a pulse. "Some men do."

They both looked at Paul, who stood way too close, his head inclined toward Marlie's as he murmured who knows what.

He wore a navy sports coat with a shirt he'd left unbuttoned instead of the white chef's coat. His hair was on the long side with a poufiness that screamed professional styling. At least that's what it screamed to Ty. He looked more like a gigolo than a chef.

Marlie didn't seem to mind. No, Marlie was all pink-cheeked and twinkling.

"Come," Paul said, before linking her arm with his. "Let me show you where to sit."

He led them to bar stools on either side of a stainless steel prep table. It was set for four and there was a single red rose in a bud vase.

A red rose? What a cliché.

"Marlene, please to sit here." Paul had positioned the prep table so that it formed an L with the gas range. Marlie would sit closest in the best spot to watch him work. Paul pulled out the bar stool and put his hand on her back to guide her toward it. Marlie swayed toward him and Ty saw Paul's hand slip downward into slapping territory.

FREE Merchandise is 'in the Cards' for you!

Dear Reader,

We're giving away FREE MERCHANDISE!

Seriously, we'd like to reward you for reading this novel by giving you **FREE MERCHANDISE** worth over **$20**. And no purchase is necessary!

You see the Jack of Hearts sticker above? Paste that sticker in the box on the Free Merchandise Voucher inside. Return the Voucher promptly...and we'll send you valuable Free Merchandise!

Thanks again for reading one of our novels—and enjoy your Free Merchandise with our compliments!

Pam Powers

Pam Powers

P.S. Look inside to see what Free Merchandise is **"in the cards"** for you!

(H-B-12/10)

YOUR FREE MERCHANDISE INCLUDES...

2 FREE Harlequin® Blaze® Books
AND 2 FREE Mystery Gifts

FREE MERCHANDISE VOUCHER

2 FREE
BOOKS
and
2 FREE
GIFTS

Please send my Free Merchandise, consisting of
2 Free Books and **2 Free Mystery Gifts**.
I understand that I am under no obligation to buy
anything, as explained on the back of this card.

*About how many NEW paperback fiction books
have you purchased in the past 3 months?*

❏ 0-2   ❏ 3-6   ❏ 7 or more
E9CY   E9DC   E9DN

151/351 HDL

Please Print

FIRST NAME

LAST NAME

ADDRESS

APT.#   CITY

STATE/PROV.   ZIP/POSTAL CODE

NO PURCHASE NECESSARY!

◄ Detach card and mail today. No stamp needed. ►

© 2010 HARLEQUIN ENTERPRISES LIMITED. ® and ™ are trademarks owned and used by the trademark owner and/or its licensee. Printed in the U.S.A.

(H-B-12/10)

He also saw Marlie neatly sidestep as she slid onto the bar stool.

That little sidestep did a lot for Ty's peace of mind. Marlie wasn't a total novice with men.

He watched her cross her legs and smile up at Paul as he poured wine into an oversized goblet.

As Marlie sipped, Paul gestured with the wine bottle to the two places on the opposite side of the table.

Ty looked at Axelle only to find her watching him thoughtfully. "Shall we?" He put his hand in the small of her back, but Axelle moved too fast and his fingers just brushed the fabric of her dress before falling away.

"Axelle tells me that you two are old friends," Paul said when they were seated.

"Our parents met in college and ended up living in San Diego. We'd take vacations together when Ty and I were growing up," Marlie answered.

"What kind of vacations?" Axelle asked.

"Long ones," Ty said.

Marlie laughed, but it wasn't a normal Marlie laugh. It was a "toss-your-hair" and "shimmy-your-shoulders" laugh.

Another flirting move Ty recognized. He'd seen women do it while sitting at bars right after they'd met a guy they were interested in. And now Marlie was doing it here. For Paul.

"Our parents liked to rent cabins at resorts and camps where there were organized children's activities. That way, they could go off and play golf or whatever and poor Ty—" Marlie sent him a look of mock sympathy "—he had to babysit me."

"Not *babysit*," he clarified so he wouldn't seem so old. "I mostly had to let her follow me around and see that she got to where she was supposed to be."

"As you did tonight." Paul wasn't looking at Ty as he said this. Oh, no. He was caressing Marlie with his eyes.

Paul raised his goblet. "To good friends and good food."

Everyone clinked glasses. What was this, a commercial for wine coolers?

Ty sipped at the white wine, immediately recognizing that it had come from the high end of Ravigote's list, costing far more than the minimum bid for the date.

But Ty hadn't paid the minimum, had he? No, Ty had bought the whole damn package just so he could be alone with this guy's sister. Only he wasn't. So by all means, let's break out the good stuff.

"Is the wine not to your liking?" Axelle asked.

"It's great," Ty answered. "Why?"

"You're glowering," she murmured.

"Am I?" Probably. He'd certainly been ignoring her. He smiled and leaned in a little. "You look beautiful tonight."

"Do I?"

Clearly, Ty needed to do some damage control. She was wearing black, which she almost always wore, and she'd slicked her hair back.

Axelle's hair was short, shorter than Ty preferred on women, and he didn't particularly like the wet, stuck to the head look, but he knew it was supposed to be stylish. "You always look beautiful," he told her.

Her expression didn't change.

Ty turned his body so he could face her. Taking a page from Paul's playbook, he leaned even closer. "If I'm 'glowering' as you put it, it's only because I would rather be alone with you tonight." He held her gaze so she could see his sincerity. Because he was really, really sincere.

At last Axelle smiled. Propping her elbows on the prep table's raised edge, she dangled her glass dangerously between both hands. A flirting move. He was back in. "Maybe when Marlie goes on her next date," she promised. "I've been training an assistant hostess. If the night is not too busy, perhaps she can take over for a few hours."

Ty's blood heated.

Axelle's smile turned knowing as she watched him over the rim of her glass.

Okay. Okay, then.

Axelle broke eye contact to look across the table and Ty became aware of Marlie chattering away. Chattering about the wine.

"...and so the difference between this vintage and the 2008 was so great, the winery felt they had to mention it on the label."

"How do you know that?" Ty asked her.

"Jason told her, most likely," Axelle said, and Marlie nodded in confirmation. "This is one of his favorite wines."

"Perhaps you could see if we have some of the 2008 left, Elle," Paul suggested to his sister. "We can make our own comparison."

"Of course." She slid off the bar stool and headed for the walk-in, climate-controlled wine cellar.

"I have prepared an *amuse-bouche* for you," Paul said to Marlie before he moved to the refrigerators, leaving Ty and Marlie alone at the table.

She waited until Paul's back was turned before baring her teeth in a huge, excited Marlie grin. "This is so cool!" she whispered. "I feel like a movie star, you know? Like I'm so famous I have to eat back here so I won't be bothered by the fans and paparazzi."

That grin got to him. How could he not feel happy when she grinned at him like that? "Glad you're enjoying yourself."

"Oh, I am. I know you probably come back here all the time, but I've never been in a restaurant kitchen before."

She looked around as Ty considered the fact that he had *not* been in the kitchen before.

"And I don't know what it is, but having a man cook for you is just so sexy. Now I know why you perfected your bouillabaisse."

"Didn't whatshisname cook for you?"

"Eric?" She shook her head. "He'd grill steaks or burgers, but not fix a whole meal."

Axelle returned, carrying two bottles, and Ty reflected that he'd already shot his entire repertoire of date dishes. He was going to have to come up with another menu. He watched Paul's approach. So what if Axelle had a brother who cooked. Maybe she was tired of his cooking.

"A small gift for you." Paul set a tiny plate in front of each of them.

"Look! It's a little package!" Marlie turned her excited face toward Paul.

He stood next to her, smiling indulgently.

"Ah, the square quail's egg is always a hit," Axelle said.

Marlie's smile dimmed and Paul's disappeared entirely as he gave his sister a long look.

She ignored him and turned to Ty. "He cooks them in molds. Not so very difficult."

Wow. Ty didn't know Axelle's brother, but you had to feel for the guy. What was up with her?

"Oh, do you cook, Axelle?" Marlie asked sweetly.

"No."

She didn't?

"I can understand why you don't when you've got a brother as spectacularly talented as Paul." Marlie beamed up at him and there was nothing indulgent about his smile now. It was a full-on I-find-you-incredibly-attractive smile.

And Marlie was smiling back.

Just when Ty was ready to say something to remind them that they weren't alone, Paul removed his suit jacket and walked around the table to the range, rolling up the sleeves of his black shirt as he went.

"Look at the little bows." Marlie touched the one on her present. "Green onions?"

"Yes." Still smiling, Paul whipped a white apron around his waist, fired up a burner, and plopped a stick of butter into a copper skillet.

And, Ty grudgingly admitted, he looked pretty macho while doing it. Okay, props to the guy for being able to pull that off.

"It's so perfect." Marlie continued to marvel over the little white cube. "I can't even tie a good bow with ribbon, let alone with vegetables."

Just eat the thing, Ty thought.

"Taste it," Paul urged her. "All at once. One bite."

"I—" Marlie bent over and retrieved her purse. Paul's eyes widened.

Marlie's neckline looked pretty spectacular from Ty's side of the table, so he could only imagine the view Paul got standing next to her.

But Ty was not going to imagine the view. In fact, Ty was going to drag his eyes away from Marlie and her neckline and pay attention to the ominously silent Axelle at his side.

Axelle's neckline was actually at her neck. But her shoulders were bare and there was a deep slit in the back. She looked sexy, but a different kind of sexy.

"You don't cook?" Ty asked her.

She gave him a hot, smoky look. "I don't have to."

She held his gaze as she slowly sipped her wine. Talk about signals.

He heard Paul chuckle as Marlie took a picture of the little package with her cell phone.

But then Marlie popped the egg into her mouth. "Mmm," she moaned, eyes closed, lips moving.

Paul stopped chuckling. He may have stopped breathing. The only sounds were butter sizzling and Marlie's little moans.

He needed to have the signal talk with Marlie, Ty thought.

"Your butter is burning," Axelle said, and Paul turned off the flame.

At least the one on the stove.

Ty ate his egg. "Mmm."

"Stop it," Axelle said. She pushed her plate to the side, her *bouche* unamused.

"Tastes good," Ty said brightly. "There's something more than just egg inside."

"I inject flavoring before the egg solidifies," Paul explained without looking away from Marlie.

"That's so clever." Marlie continued being Paul's personal cheerleader. "Was that your idea?"

"Yes." He drew out the word as he slowly stirred a sauce that had been simmering since they'd arrived.

The guy sure had moves, Ty would give him that.

Marlie seemed hypnotized by his hand. "How did you ever think of it?"

Paul took a spoon, dipped it into the sauce, and leaned on his elbows offering Marlie a taste. "I like to experiment."

Marlie opened her mouth and he dribbled sauce on her tongue.

Ty was going to have to remember that trick.

She laughed softly and his eyes grew heavy-lidded as she swallowed and licked her lips. "Yum," she said.

They gazed at each other. Again.

Ty could practically see heat waves coming off them and technically, they hadn't even been served the first course yet. Just a pre-appetizer.

Marlie was playing in the big leagues, here. This guy was

something else. Mouth dry, Tyler reached for his wine glass only to discover that it was empty. Wine. He needed wine. "Weren't we going to compare vintages?" he asked Axelle in a voice that was too loud.

"Indeed we were." She picked up a waiter's corkscrew and expertly opened a second bottle.

Getting another set of glasses and pouring everyone tastes of the two wines cooled off the mutual lovefest between Marlie and Paul, not that Ty cared if they made goo-goo eyes at each other.

Marlie could make goo-goo eyes at whomever she wanted and if she chose to make them at a French hound dog who happened to be able to cook, it was nothing to Ty.

Which was a good thing because that's what they did for the rest of the evening. For some reason, Paul, a renowned chef, seemed unable to cook without Marlie tasting every step of the way and signaling her passionate approval.

He had a knack of positioning the spoon or fork or, in one memorable instance, his fingers, in a way that caused Marlie to lean forward and tilt her head back with a mesmerizing display of her throat and chest. Each time she stretched, Tyler swore her top revealed a fraction of an inch more white skin. And not just any skin, but breast skin.

The top of her dress went straight across and the little strappy sleeve things at the far edge of her shoulders weren't doing much to hold up the middle. She was dangerously close to wardrobe malfunction territory.

He was barely aware of Axelle slipping away and reappearing on the other side of the table to murmur in Paul's ear. To do so, she had to stand right next to Marlie and Ty unwillingly compared the two women.

Axelle was tall and thin and darkly exotic. His type.

Marlie was creamy and lush. And jiggled. Not his type.

Right then Marlie's gaze connected with his and his blood began to simmer.

Why? Why is she not your type?

He couldn't remember.

8

TYLER LOOKED ACROSS THE TABLE at Marlie with that stern expression he'd worn all evening. It bugged her, so she ignored him to flirt with Paul, who sent her hot looks even though he had blue eyes.

American men didn't look at her the way Paul did. They couldn't pull off the bold sensuality without it appearing ridiculous or sleazy. When Paul looked at her, Marlie knew he was thinking about sex, and not just any sex, but a lingering sensual exploration of her body... She shivered, ready to hand him a map.

Maybe it had something to do with his mouth. His lips were remarkably full. Marlie was fascinated by those lips, what they'd feel like on hers and on her body. Ty's lips were pulled taut and thin with disapproval. He could keep his lips.

Clearly, Paul was a master of seduction. He wasn't even trying, not that he'd have to try hard with her, what with the way he moved... She sighed. The man's tailor was a genius. Why didn't American men's slacks fit that way? Then there was his deep voice with that accent, the fascinating cleft in his chin, and the fact that he was cooking for her.... Marlie sighed again, very glad she was a woman.

Maybe she'd just stay with Paul tonight and Ty could take Axelle home.

Everybody would win.

"The food is not ready for plating!" Paul said loud enough to bring Marlie out of her sensual haze.

"Just plate one serving. Alicia Hartson is on her way over right now." Axelle gripped his arm. "Think of the publicity, Paul!"

Paul flung off her hand. "And while she is here taking her pictures, the rest of the food will be ruined. The sauce will overcook and the chicken will get cold!" He added something in French. Brother and sister glared at each other.

"It's okay," Marlie stood and looked across the table. Ty had been very quiet. For once, he was looking at Axelle and not at her, but he didn't appear any happier.

"Ty?" His eyes swiveled toward her. "Help me clear away the extra glasses and dishes."

His brows drew together.

"The reporter will want to have a nice backdrop for the taping," Marlie explained to him and the glaring siblings. "I've been through this twice now. I know the drill."

"Gotcha." He moved the bottles to another cart.

"Clean glasses?" Marlie asked Axelle. "We don't want lip prints or smudges." Axelle pointed.

Marlie got fresh napkins while she was at it and by the time Alicia Hartson and her cameraman arrived, the setting looked as much like a magazine cover as Marlie could make it.

Because, after all this was over, Ravigote was still her web client. She had a vested interest in anything that boosted the restaurant's business.

The interruption sure killed the mood, though. Probably not a bad thing since she and Paul had taken flirting as far as it could go in public, especially when the public was his sister and Marlie's parental-acting roommate.

In spite of Paul's concern, the food was not ruined, although Marlie might have been influenced by extreme hunger. Paul and Axelle were extremely photogenic and Alicia Hartson spent enough time in Ravigote's kitchen to tape a documentary. Even Ty was included, as the purchaser of the date. He didn't say much, though. Marlie knew him well enough to know something was bothering him, but she couldn't figure out what.

And, to be completely and totally honest, she was having too much fun with Paul to concern herself with Ty's dark mood.

The man was a walking talking French cliché. He had a bit of a temper, probably a big temper, but for the most part, he kept it in check. All that energy had to go somewhere and right now, it was put to flirting and being sexy and making Marlie feel sexy and womanly. Womanly, as in making every part of her aware that she was female and he was male and he liked that about her. He reveled in it and invited her to revel in it, too. He was sensual, and made Marlie realize that she hadn't been living a sensual life. Sex was only part of it, which by the way, she was keenly aware of living without, as well. But Paul, hot though he was, seduced all the senses. Obviously taste and smell, inviting her to enjoy the steps that went into the lovely food he prepared, and sight, because he didn't just plop the food on a plate; he artfully and whimsically arranged it. She smiled when she remembered the square quail egg present.

There wasn't music playing in the kitchen, but he used his deep voice, with the alluring accent, to charm her. Then there was touch. Ah. Paul was the touchy sort, holding her chin as he fed her bites of food, using his fingers to check seasoning and actually offering her a quick taste by letting her lick one.

And the amazing thing was that it didn't seem awkward or hokey at all. It was just right for the moment.

And the food was absolutely incredible.

The promised chicken three ways consisted of a layered chicken terrine with a chipotle sauce. Paul had made it in the shape of a chicken, which Marlie sliced open on camera to reveal flavored layers inside. The second way was a roasted hen covered in saucy goodness, but the third way was her favorite. Nachos. But not any nachos. The chips were pieces of crispy fried chicken skin and he'd topped them with some gooey French cheese and peppers. Texas-Continental fusion at its best.

If anyone had ever told her she'd crave chicken skin, she'd have thought they were crazy. All those years of cutting off the fatty skin because it was bad for you—what a waste. Calories? Who cared about calories?

Marlie was on sensual overload and ready for something or someone to flip her safety valve.

Paul. He'd make her forget she had a safety valve. And as a bonus, he'd probably cook her breakfast.

They were at the end of the meal. He sat next to her, fist propping his jaw, watching as she ate the last of some incredible chocolatey dessert. She licked her lips and sent him a "take-me-now" look, just in case he had any lingering doubts about her availability.

He chuckled and murmured, "Did you enjoy your dinner, *ma petite?*"

"Oh, yes. I'm sorry it has to end." Which was his cue to lean close and whisper that it didn't have to end *quite* yet.

He smiled, a soft, fond smile. "I am so glad I've made you happy."

Yes, but she could be happier. Much happier. He could be happier, too. *Every*body could be happier.

Paul raised his water glass and said, "I believe we can count

Three French Hens a success." He gestured across the table in a toast and the others raised their glasses, too. Because, oh, yes, Ty and Axelle were still there, although Marlie had forgotten about them. Why hadn't Ty taken Axelle away?

"Ma petite?" Paul raised his eyebrows at her, his eyes warm and friendly.

Oh. Okay. She got it. Marlie picked up her glass. She was also drinking water, since she'd had her limit of wine a while back. She'd wanted no accusations of drunken behavior from Mr. Killjoy across the table. "To Chef Paul, for the best meal I've eaten in my entire life." It may have been. It may not have been. But that wasn't the point, Marlie understood as Paul inclined his head to accept everyone's praise.

The point was that he'd called her *"ma petite"* which meant he didn't see her as a potential bed partner. And the hot looks of earlier had been banked to a fond glow.

In other words, he'd been acting. Putting on a show, she realized. Not out of malice or to lead her on, but simply because it added to the enjoyment of the moment.

But the moment was ending and Marlie knew she'd never see him again unless she came to eat at his restaurant, which she couldn't afford. Or, she thought darkly, as she looked across the table, if Ty married Axelle and Marlie ran into Paul at the wedding.

Assuming she'd be invited.

ACROSS THE TABLE, Ty saw the look Marlie gave Paul. No. Seriously? *Seriously?* She couldn't tell the guy was just playing her?

Or…she knew and didn't care?

Sure, maybe she didn't care now, when she was caught up in all the attention he'd been giving her, but in the morning she would. Marlie would want to snuggle and talk about the kind of drawer pulls and the right wood for their future home, but Paul would callously send her on her way with a cup of coffee and a cold croissant that he probably hadn't even made himself.

The thought of Marlie in her bright red dress having to call a cab, or worse, call him, because Axelle's brother thought he was too busy and too important to take her home, made Ty grit his teeth.

Marlie wasn't the one-night-stand type. She was looking for love and marriage and this guy wasn't. So far, she hadn't picked up on that.

Tyler set his glass down and turned to Axelle. She saw what was happening, didn't she? Axelle met his gaze as she sipped water and then went back to observing her brother and Marlie.

She knew.

Ty stood and offered her his hand, ignoring the question in her eyes until he'd led her into the darkened dining room.

"What is it?" Axelle pressed the switch that lit the area next to the door, leaving the rest of the room in darkness.

"You've got to say something to your brother."

"What about?"

She knew what about. "Tell him to leave Marlie alone."

"Why?" Axelle crossed her arms, clearly not a woman who responded to orders.

"Because he's just playing with her. I don't want her to get hurt," Ty said.

"Marlie won't get hurt. She can't possibly believe he would ever be interested in a real relationship with her."

Ty didn't like the way that sounded. "Why wouldn't Paul be interested in a relationship with her?" he asked, forgetting that he didn't want that either. "She's smart, she comes from good people, she's easy to live with, and on top of that, she's a total babe."

Axelle made a sound in the back of her throat. "She lacks sophistication."

"Paul wasn't exactly staring at her sophistication."

Axelle lifted her shoulder in a dismissive shrug. "Yes, she's very obvious."

"Obviously what?"

"Her type will always appeal to less discerning men." She looked him directly in the eyes. "To you, perhaps."

Ty took a step backwards. "Marlie is a long-time friend, Axelle."

"Friend, is it?" Her voice rose. "I saw the way you looked at her. All during dinner, you stared at her. I might as well have not been in the room."

"You're jealous!" And if she was jealous, that meant she cared about him. Ty instantly forgave her for trading a night alone with him for a publicity opportunity. "You're jealous of Marlie!" He could kiss Marlie and her blond head.

"I certainly am not!" Axelle snapped.

But he laughed and hugged her stiff body to him. "Come on," he said. "Let's go rescue Marlie from your brother."

"WE WERE HAVING ESPRESSO," Marlie grumbled for the eightieth time since they'd left the restaurant. "You didn't even let Paul put on my charm!"

"You'd had enough of Paul's charm."

"I can't believe you came swooping in as if you were my father and you'd caught Paul and me necking on the front porch!"

"More than your neck was involved!" When Ty and Axelle had returned to the kitchen, they'd found Paul bent over Marlie with one hand traveling up her thigh and his tongue down her throat, not that Ty had actually seen Paul's tongue, but he was familiar with the technique.

"You completely humiliated me!" She stormed up the

stairs, switched on the light and kept going until she was in the kitchen.

Ty climbed the steps. Marlie in angry motion was something to see and Ty enjoyed seeing it. Lots of jiggling. So he was a man who lacked refinement. What else was new?

She was mad at him. He'd overreacted, but he'd done so in her best interests. He'd apologized. Multiple times. He was finished apologizing for that. There was bound to be something new to apologize for before the string of dates was over.

Marlie dropped her purse on the counter and opened the junk drawer. Grabbing the needle-nosed pliers, she attacked the tiny silver charm Paul had given her.

"Ow!" She grabbed her hand. "Now look what you made me do!"

"I made you pinch yourself?"

"Yes!"

They both knew he hadn't, but Ty apologized anyway. See? He'd known there'd be something else. "Let me have the charm." He held out his hand.

"No!"

"Come on, Marlie. Don't be childish."

"I wasn't childish earlier and you didn't like that, either."

"Marlie." Exasperated, he grabbed for her hand. Marlie jerked away from him and then gasped as the charm went flying. A second later, a faint ping sounded. "Now look what you've done!"

Ty closed his eyes. He was going to remember this moment the next time he was struck with the urge to be nice. Then he opened his eyes to see Marlie on her hands and knees, face near the floor, butt in the air, looking for the charm.

He was going to remember this moment, too.

She was killing him. He sighed deeply and dropped to the floor to help her look for the charm.

"This floor is filthy," she said. "I don't suppose it ever occurred to you to get out the mop."

"Guilty," he said. "I'll pay for half if you want to hire a house-cleaning service." He could be reasonable.

Marlie could not. "We don't need a house-cleaning service. We need you to run the vacuum around or grab a dust rag every once in a while."

"Okay, but the house never seems to get that dirty."

"Why do you think that is? The house fairies?" She tilted her head up to give him a murderous glance that was totally spoiled by how good her breasts looked. They were squeezed upward by her dress and with Marlie on all fours, gravity added a bonus special effect. He was really a fan of gravity right now.

"Ty?" she asked dangerously.

"Mmm?"

"Are you looking down my dress?"

Hell. "Yes. Yes, I am."

"And you see nothing wrong with looking down my dress?"

"Nope. Everything looks good."

Slowly she straightened and sat back on her heels. Her breasts jostled into place, mounding softly above her neckline. He waited until the last ripple was over before focusing on the way her dress stretched tightly across her thighs. She looked like an old-fashioned pin-up girl, except for the angry expression.

"And yet you had a problem when Paul looked down my dress."

"You *knew* Paul was looking down your dress?"

She rolled her eyes.

"Marlie... He's...he's—"

"Axelle's brother?"

Ty ran his hand through his hair when he really wanted to

punch something. "He's a player. He was just out for what he could get."

"Hmm." Marlie sighed. "He could have had a lot."

Ty knew. Everybody knew. "He's not serious about you."

She got very quiet. Ty had been harsh, but better she get her feelings bruised now than her heart broken again later.

"So that's why you didn't like him looking down my dress? Because he's not serious?"

"Yes." Finally, she understood. He exhaled in relief.

His relief was short lived.

"You were looking down my dress," she said, thoughtfully. "Does that mean you're serious?"

He was toast.

Ty stared unblinking. There was no easy way out of this. "It's not the same."

"Oh? Help me understand why Paul looking is bad, but you looking is okay." She crossed her arms.

He wished she hadn't done that. He willed himself to maintain eye contact. "He's French."

"Seriously."

"I'm pretty sure. He's got an accent."

"You're worse than he is!"

Worse? Worse than a man who would take what he wanted and drop her like a hot croissant? "That is not true."

"At least Paul is open about appreciating a woman's body instead of being sneaky!"

Sneaky? She made him sound like he'd drilled a hole in the girl's locker room. "Pardon me for looking out for you—"

"You're looking all right."

"Marlie—" Ty broke off. He was angry and frustrated and didn't want to say something he'd regret. "You want to fling yourself at Paul, fine. Go ahead. But I can't figure out what you see in the guy."

"He makes me feel like a natural woman," she said in a sing-songy voice.

"What I saw when Axelle and I came back into the kitchen did not look natural."

"It's his mouth," Marlie said and Ty remembered the way hers looked when she said, *"Poulet."* His own mouth tightened.

"Paul's lips are full and sensual and he says the loveliest things." She narrowed her eyes. "Yours are looking a little thin, especially with the expression you've got now. Like you're a dried-up prune who can't stand to see anyone having fun. And that's the way you looked. All. Night. Long." She uncrossed her arms and pushed herself back on her knees. "You know what? I can't figure out what Axelle sees in you."

She'd found his weak spot. Axelle was the ultimate in the type of woman Ty usually went for, but he felt her slipping away. Because of Marlie. And right now, looking at Marlie, he did not care.

Which was dangerous, for both of them.

Marlie was still talking as she looked for her charm beneath the stove and along the baseboards under the cabinets—but Ty was no longer listening. It was the same pattern—Marlie interfering with his love life because Ty was responsible for making sure she didn't get hurt.

Look what happened when he hadn't been around—she got tangled up with Eric. And when he saw her about to make the same mistake again and tried to steer her away, she yelled at him.

She'd never yelled at him before.

She'd never turned him on before, either.

The more he tried to suppress his desire, the stronger it grew.

She walked toward him on her knees, flipped her hair

over her shoulder and held it back as she bent to run her hand beneath the dishwasher.

Her dress had slithered up her thighs. Of course he'd stared at her. That was the whole point of that dress and he remembered telling her so. He was a man. He responded like a man and there was no way she could be unaware of the effect she had on him. He tried to be decent and she called him sneaky.

As she crawled forward, Marlie's knee caught the hem of her dress and pulled at the neckline. Ty held his breath. Absently she straightened to tug it back into place and glanced at him, catching his transfixed stare.

She stopped moving, or most of her did. It was the damn jiggling. Ty wasn't used to women who jiggled. Marlie left her thumbs anchored beneath the fabric's edge, but her fingers relaxed their hold and fanned out over skin. Caressing. Inviting. Then she smiled a little self-satisfied, smirky smile, tugged her dress upward and resumed her search for the charm.

Ty could feel the blood pounding in his ears. His body wanted her, but his mind didn't.

Actually, his mind was coming around as he watched her mouth move, watched her back arch, and looked down her dress again.

And then, he just let go. He let go of his memory of little-girl Marlie and let the image of grown-up woman Marlie take her place.

He enjoyed a few seconds of relief before hot, sexy Marlie shoved grown-up Marlie out of the way and said, "Come and get me, big boy."

Ty took the brakes off his desire and it raced through him.

Angry Marlie-on-the-kitchen-floor was completely unaware of the cataclysmic shift in their relationship.

She looked up, and then straightened. "Is that all you plan to do? Stare down my dress? Or are you going to help me fi—"

Ty planted his hands on either side of her face and kissed her.

He hadn't planned to kiss her, hadn't even thought about kissing her. He hadn't allowed himself. He'd just acknowledged a general desire that he had no intention of acting on, and refused to dwell on specifics.

Except while his mind had been keeping things fuzzy, his body had been very clear about what it wanted and who it wanted it with.

Marlie.

That was the shocker. He wasn't supposed to want Marlie. He never dreamed he'd want Marlie. And yet here she was, almost, but not quite, in his arms. And he wanted her so very, very much.

He slid one hand from her cheek over miles of smooth, soft skin to her back and pulled her against him. Actually, her bare knees didn't slide on the kitchen tile, but his pants-covered ones did. Whatever worked. She was in his arms and his mouth was open on hers and since he hadn't anticipated ever being in this situation with her, he didn't have a plan. So he was going to wing it.

Kissing her would be a good place to begin.

Except it seemed that Marlie had started without him.

He felt a gentle tug on his lower lip and the tip of her tongue brushed across it. Heat washed over his skin, a prickly dry heat that woke up every cell and said, "Hang on. This is going to be good."

Tilting his head, Ty leaned closer, softening his lips, moving them against hers, where they fit, oh-so-perfectly.

He tasted a lingering earthiness from the espresso with an underlying spiciness that was all Marlie. He'd expected sweet. And shy. Sweet, shy, good-girl Marlie—whose tongue was now boldly stroking his. He shuddered. Sweet. And good, really good.

Her arms linked around his waist as she worked herself closer until they were pressed together from shoulder to knee. Her lush breasts pillowed his chest and her thighs invited him to sink into her. Part of him had already RSVPed.

Marlie had a plan and a good one, which meant she'd been thinking about this—about them. Together. The realization sent another wave of heat over him, burning away any lingering reservations he had about kissing her.

He slipped his tongue into her mouth, determined to give her the hottest, deepest, heart-poundingest kiss in the history of kisses. The kiss to obliterate the memory of any kiss she'd ever had, along with whoever had been doing the kissing. The kiss to redefine kissing.

The kiss she'd been waiting for her whole life.

9

MARLIE HAD BEEN SO ANGRY at Ty. It was an anger fueled by the frustration of a three-year dry spell and two men determined to save her from herself. A few seconds more and she could have convinced Paul that she wasn't so petite after all, but no. Ty had come charging into the kitchen, shocked, *shocked* at what he'd seen. He'd treated her as though she were a teenager out with the grownups for the first time and flirting embarrassingly with a friend of her father's.

She was not a teenager and Ty needed to stop seeing her as one. Honestly, they'd gotten along great until he'd decided to buy the dates for her.

Paul would have been a great lover, perfect for testing the equipment and making sure everything still worked. Maybe even tweaking a few things here and there. Kind of a tune-up before a long road trip. A night with him would have been about mutual pleasure and nothing else. But it would have been *all* about pleasure. However, Marlie hadn't been pleased, and she'd been left all twitchy and full of restless energy. Worse, the bed she'd bought this morning wasn't going to be delivered until Friday. Not only that, but Ty had lost her charm, an expensive one that had three hens with ruby eyes sitting on a banner that actually said, "Three French Hens."

Then, instead of helping her look for it, he kissed her.

Kissed her three ways to Sunday, actually.

She hadn't seen it coming and knew he hadn't either, because he'd just grabbed her, and then stayed frozen with his mouth open on hers. Marlie didn't know who was more surprised that they'd locked lips, but she recovered first. She figured Ty was waiting for some signal from her that she was okay with him kissing her. So she did her best to let him know she was more than okay. He took over from there.

For two people who didn't like each other, the chemistry between them was incredible. Then Marlie remembered that she did like him now, and the kiss got even better. Why hadn't they done this years ago? They'd wasted so much time. Being in Ty's arms felt so right, it was scary good. Ty was kissing her as though he'd never kiss her again, as if this one moment was all they'd ever have. Oh, no. They were going to have moments. More moments. And they were going to have them tonight.

TY POURED EVERYTHING he had into kissing Marlie, starting with his recent sexual frustration, which had just added to the general frustration he'd felt with her for as long as he'd known her. He'd always wanted to be somewhere else, doing something else, with someone else, but there she'd been—stuck to him.

She was stuck to him now, but Ty didn't want to be anywhere else, doing anything else, with anyone else.

He breathed into her and inhaled the mingled air deep into his lungs until he was dizzy. Their mouths moved together so naturally that Ty didn't have to think or plan or analyze whether what he was doing was working or not. He was winging it and everything was perfect.

They'd connected in a way he'd never experienced. And it was just a kiss. Imagining more overloaded his brain. He sucked gently on her lip and when she mimicked him, he felt the tug all the way down in his groin. His fingers threaded through her silky hair and he smiled against her mouth, thinking how much harder it would have been to comb them through her frizzy curls.

Marlie arched her neck and Ty pressed open-mouthed kisses to her jaw and below, settling on the pulse he felt beating against his lips. He sucked lightly, not wanting to mar the creamy, white skin, breathing in her scent, recognizing Marlie beneath the unfamiliar chemicals in the cosmetics and whatever she'd used on her hair.

He wanted to taste her. Ty licked her skin, and Marlie gave a small gasp that flared Ty's desire as though the tiny sound was a lit match tossed into a pool of gasoline.

This kiss had just become more than a kiss and he didn't care. Moving his hands over her shoulders, he pushed at the little sleeves that weren't doing anything except covering her skin, her smooth, soft, delectable skin.

He ran his fingers against the neckline across her back and teased his thumbs against the tight edge at her shoulders, the tight, very tight edge that stretched straight across her front, except for the tiniest gap between her swelling breasts.

That gap became his focus, his goal. He was going for the gap.

Ty kissed his way to the sweet spot just above her collarbone and heard her breathing quicken, noticing vaguely that it was in sync with his. He pressed his thumbs into the skin at the front of her shoulders, hoping to slip beneath the tight edge, but the stretchy fabric stuck to her.

Okay, that didn't work.

Marlie "mmmmed" encouragingly and grabbed his butt, which gave him an idea. Actually lots of ideas, but for now, he went with the one that had him returning the favor by grabbing one of her red-fabric-covered hips and holding her close. He drew his knuckles from her shoulder over the gentle rise of one breast and paused at the shallow dip between the other rise.

He tucked a finger into the gap and Marlie trembled. Ty closed his eyes because, glued together as they were, Marlie's trembling caused some seriously good vibrations.

He tugged against the dress's tight line of defense as he kissed his way to the gap his finger had failed to widen.

Marlie inhaled deeply and Ty remembered the dress inching downward. Downward when her knee caught it. Downward as she tasted Paul's stupid spoonfuls of food, but not downward when Ty had his fingers tugging on the edge.

So he took his fingers away and substituted his tongue, delving into the gap as far as he could, tracing tantalizing curves...

"Ty..." Marlie breathed, clutching his head to her.

He skimmed one hand over her breast, but felt nothing, reacting only because he knew the flesh beneath the red armor was breast flesh and not stomach or thigh or elbow flesh. Which were all good fleshes, except maybe the elbow.

But they were not breast flesh and that's what he wanted to touch. From the way Marlie was squirming against him, she wanted it, too.

He kissed his way back to her mouth, his fingers spreading the moisture left by his tongue in hopes the neckline would slide down.

And it did. Maybe a half inch. He could measure, if he wanted, since it left an angry red line across her chest.

There had been no line earlier. Then again, earlier, she hadn't been hunting around on all fours. Gravity, previously his friend, had left the neckline with more of Marlie to contain, and contain it did.

Ty was not going to get into an undignified struggle with Marlie's red dress on the kitchen floor. No, he was going to draw her to her feet, lead her upstairs to his room, and peel the thing off her. That was the plan. Ty always was better with plans.

Ty raised his mouth from Marlie's. He looked into her flushed face with her lips rosy from his kisses and was ready to put the plan into action.

"Mmm, Ty..." She threw back her head, shrugged her shoulders and inhaled deeply.

The neckline of the dress surrendered, slipping, slipping, until the blood thundered in Ty's ears and the air left his lungs and his hand was the only thing holding up the fabric.

He saw Marlie's mouth form his name. Saw her bite her lower lip. Felt her rock her hips against his. He lifted his hand and watched the dress whisper over her nipples.

Lust slammed into him.

Perfect creamy breasts, larger than he'd expected, and all Marlie. No magic bra with pads that boosted curves. In fact, no bra at all.

She'd gone out dressed like that? All evening, when Paul had been standing over her and Marlie had been stretching and the neckline had been slipping, there had been nothing but naked Marlie flesh beneath it?

Ty flashed to Paul's hand traveling up Marlie's thigh. Was she wearing *anything* under this dress? Spots formed behind his eyelids and he gasped a much-needed breath.

"You—you've got the most beautiful breasts I've ever seen," he blurted out, glad he still had enough control to say "breasts" instead of tits, boobs, or cha-chas. And then blew it by adding, "In person."

Marlie's throaty laugh was unlike any Marlie laugh he'd ever heard. "Your jacket is scratchy."

"Oh." He whipped it off and tossed it behind her, thinking it would provide some padding against the floor.

Which was the last complete, rational thought he had as

Marlie's fingers began working the buttons on his shirt. He couldn't wait for her slow, cold fingers, so he pulled the whole thing over his head, impatiently jerking the buttoned cuffs past his wrists. He inhaled sharply when her cold fingers touched his skin, but as her hands moved over his chest, he realized it wasn't cold he felt, but heat.

Ty was on fire for her. He quickly kissed her mouth, her throat, the top of her breast and teased her nipple with his lips, dimly hearing her whispered, "Yes," as he tugged it into his mouth. With each stroke of his tongue, she squirmed against him, stoking the flames. Ty smoothed his palm down her back to her thigh. As he swept his hand upward beneath the hem, the dress rolled out of his way. All he encountered was bare skin which nearly killed him until his suddenly clumsy fingers registered material so thin, it might as well have not been there at all.

He raised his head so he could lower her onto his jacket and get rid of his pants and her non-underwear, not necessarily in that order.

Lying there, hair fanned out around her head, Marlie looked as though she was wearing a large, stretchy belt and nothing else. Belt. Right. He dragged air into his lungs and fumbled with his buckle like an overeager teenager. Except when he'd been a teenager, he couldn't have imagined that someday, he'd feel desperately close to exploding at the thought of sex with Marlie. Marlie, of all people. Marlie, for years his annoying friend, was now half-naked on the kitchen floor. Soon to be all naked.

Marlie slowly opened passion-filled brown eyes and locked her all-seeing gaze with his. She'd always been able to see through him, to know what he was thinking. That gaze had been his conscience. She never had to say a word. Knowing he'd have to face that look of hers made him do the right thing, even when he didn't want to.

Ty's fingers stilled as he stared down at her. He was about to have sex with Marlie. *Marlie.* And then what? What happened next? More sex? Excruciating awkwardness? The end of a friendship or...

Ty was having a very big problem with the "or" part. He knew Marlie wanted a husband and kids, had even told her to find a man who was ready. Was he ready? Was he even that man? Did he want to be that man for her? Did he want Marlie to be that woman for him? Together forever?

He didn't know. And until he knew, until he was absolutely certain what he wanted, until he had time to *think,* this had to stop. He owed it to both of them.

Marlie levered herself off the floor and reached for his buckle. "Forget what you were doing?"

Ty captured her hands and drew a deep, ragged breath. "Yeah."

COMBUSTIBLE CHEMISTRY. A sizzling, heart-pounder of a kiss. A touch that had every molecule in Marlie's body jumping up and down, yelling, "Yes! We like him! Can we keep him?"

She'd suspected how good it could be between them, but she didn't know if Ty had.

He knew now.

Definitely not ready for a wife and kids, he'd said. *Find someone who's ready.* Did this mean he was ready?

Marlie searched his face. She'd pressed herself against him, felt the hard bulge below his waist and thought for sure she wouldn't be sleeping on the couch tonight. Then, just when things were getting interesting, he'd stopped, looking stunned. And now the hard bulge was just a bulge. Actually, more like a lump, and lumps didn't lie.

He didn't want her. She saw it in his eyes.

Marlie jerked her hands from his and deliberately pulled

her dress into place. As she did so, his gaze never left hers. The desire in his eyes faded and regret took its place.

Marlie was not *not* going to give her heart to a man who regretted something as wonderful as what they'd just shared; who could walk away from such obvious potential. Ty had a piece of her heart, he always had. But she wasn't going to give him the rest and keep herself from loving someone else.

He was watching her, trying to figure out what she was thinking when he should be trying to figure out his own thoughts. Ty drew a breath. If he apologized for kissing her, she was going to flatten his lump.

"I didn't plan this," he said.

Not exactly an apology. For now, his lump was safe.

"I'm not sure what happened," he continued.

"We kissed," Marlie reminded him. "You had me half-undressed, spread-eagled on the floor."

He winced. "I have no idea what I was thinking."

This was worse than an apology. "You were thinking we were about to have sex. I know, because that's what I was thinking."

Red stained his cheeks and throat. "Not a good idea."

"You thought it was a good idea a few seconds ago."

"I changed my mind."

"Yeah. I get that a lot." Marlie pushed her dress down her thighs. "Paul changed his mind, my fiancé changed his mind. What I want to know is, why did you change your mind?"

He had not said one nice thing to her. He'd kissed her until her knees would have given way if she hadn't already been kneeling on the floor, and now he was looking at her as though he was afraid she was going to pick out wedding china. Or cry. Or cry *while* picking out wedding china.

His mouth worked. "It wouldn't be fair to Axelle," he said, clearly relieved to have a plausible reason.

"Oh, please. Like you were thinking of Axelle."

"Marlie!" When Ty said her name, his fists clenched and unclenched. He was probably unaware of it.

"She's not right for you and you both know it."

"She *is* right for me."

So stubborn. "Why? Because she's tall and boney and cultured?"

Ty stared hard at her, breathing shallowly, visibly fighting for control of his emotions. "There's a lot more to it than that."

Marlie wanted him to give in to his emotions. "You're right. There is. So tell me, Ty, when you kiss her, do you feel one-tenth of what you just felt with me?"

No. Marlie briefly saw the answer in his face until denial chased it away.

"What I felt is not the point."

"It's *exactly* the point."

He shook his head. "This was…I don't know what it was. A fluke. We got carried away. It didn't mean anything."

"Oh." Why didn't he just stab her in the heart and get it over with?

After a couple of seconds, he continued, "And luckily, nothing happened, so we can just…"

"Forget about it?"

"Yes," he said on a relieved exhale.

Relieved that she understood. Oh, Marlie understood, all right. She understood that Ty was exactly like Eric, her ex—willing to trade away what he had, no matter how wonderful, in case he missed a chance at something better. Not actually something better, for the *chance* there *might* be something better.

But it wasn't Axelle, no matter what he said. Axelle's appeal was that she was wrong for Ty, guaranteeing their relationship would fail so he could move on to someone else. Someone who wasn't Marlie.

That was the part she had to remember—the not-Marlie part. At some point in the past, Ty had decided she wasn't his type and nothing was going to change his mind.

No matter how wrong he was, Marlie was not going to try to change it. And she wasn't waiting around for him to come to his senses, either.

He was looking at her, his expression a combination of dread, guilt, maybe even a little panic. But most of all, he looked as though he wished the last few minutes had never happened. She, however, was glad those minutes had happened. At least she knew that there would never be anything but friendship—make that a frosty friendship—between them.

"It's forgotten," she told him, pushing herself to her feet. "Never happened."

Ty was still on his knees. Yeah. He should stay there. "So... we're good then?"

We could have been. "Same as always." Marlie forced a smile and headed for the stairs.

EXCEPT THEY WEREN'T the same as always, and there was no way either of them was going to forget what happened, he knew.

So tell me, Ty, when you kiss her, do you feel one-tenth of what you just felt with me?

No. And the knowledge had Ty shivering and burning up at the same time, as if he were coming down with a fever. A Marlie fever.

Kissing her had shattered Ty's ideas about himself and what he wanted in life, and he needed to let the pieces settle before he could fit everything back together.

Maybe that's what he should have told her instead of insisting that even though they'd been so hot for each other that they'd been about to do it *on the kitchen floor,* it hadn't meant anything. Instead of letting her walk up the stairs.

That kind of blind lust just did not happen to Tyler. Oh, he wanted it to, but he wanted it with someone else. Once he found that kind of mindless passion, he wanted it to last, and from what he'd seen among his friends, kids and suburbia pretty much killed it.

He looked up the stairs and briefly considered following her to explain, except he couldn't tell Marlie he believed settling down killed passion. He didn't even like admitting it to himself. Besides, it was late, he was tired, and his knee hurt. He'd talk to her tomorrow.

Ty got off the floor, reached down to brush at his slacks, and saw a silver glint. He'd been kneeling on Marlie's charm.

Three French hens with ruby eyes. He checked for damage and it seemed to have survived. As he used the pliers to attach it to the bracelet Marlie'd left on the counter, he hoped their friendship survived, too.

10

TYLER MISSED SEEING Marlie the next morning—by the time he got up, she was in her office with the door closed.

When he arrived home from work, Marlie and her date were just leaving. Instead of driving around the corner into the alley garage entrance, Ty pulled up to the front curb behind a black muscle car and intercepted them.

The two were already holding hands, presumably because Marlie needed help walking in the high-heeled boots she wore with a pair of skin-tight jeans.

Ty was willing to bet she could walk by herself just fine. He was also willing to bet that she hadn't owned those jeans yesterday. Probably not the boots, either.

Her date looked as though he'd hit the jackpot.

Tyler got out of his car. "Hi."

Marlie gave him a cool look. "Hi." She said something to her date and he laughed and slung his arm around her. They both looked at Ty.

"So…colly birds?" Ty said, trying not to notice the way Marlie had kind of melted against the guy.

Marlie shook her head. "This is Ben, the gymnast. Five Golden Rings."

He and Ben nodded at each other. Ty tried to give the guy

an "I'm-watching-you" look, but Ben barely made eye contact before refocusing on Marlie.

"Colly birds isn't free until the weekend and Ben has tickets to Cirque du Soleil tonight. Three ring circus, get it?" Marlie giggled and touched Ben's arm. His eyes gleamed.

Ty didn't point out that Cirque wasn't a three-ring circus and there were supposed to be five golden rings, anyway. He knew what Marlie was doing. She was trying to get to him.

Ben was not the guy to toy with. They'd met, what? Five minutes ago? And his overly-muscled arm was already hanging off her, his hand dangling way too close to certain parts of Marlie Ty was trying to forget.

"I need to borrow Marlie for a minute," he said.

Marlie narrowed her eyes but extricated herself from Ben and walked over to Ty. Behind her, Ben checked out her backside.

"Marlie, I know you're mad at me—"

"I'm not mad at you."

He didn't believe her. "Good. That's good, because I wouldn't want you to do something really stupid to get back at me and get hurt in the process."

She gave him the old Marlie blank expression surrounded by the new Marlie hair, which somehow made it worse. "Tyler. It was a kiss and a little groping. I realize guys have massive egos, but it wasn't that big a deal."

Which is essentially what he'd said. Except he didn't like hearing Marlie say it. "Fair enough. But I still don't like the way that guy is looking at you."

"And how is that?" She glanced over her shoulder and waggled her fingers at Mr. Golden Rings.

"He's going to make a play for you and he'll come on strong. Be careful."

She widened her eyes. "Oh, you mean a man might actually

want to sleep with me? And here I've been thinking I'm such a troll you had to *buy* me dates."

"You know that's not true." Ty looked over her shoulder at Ben, who had the face of a man making very specific plans for the night *after* the date. "I'm telling you, right now, that guy intends to end up either at your place or his."

She gave a short laugh. "Well, we know it can't be here. Thanks for the heads up." She spun around and walked—no, sashayed—back to Ben.

Ty stared after her swaying hips. Okay, he was done. Marlie Waters could do whatever she wanted to do. Not his concern. Not his responsibility.

Raising his hand in farewell, not that they noticed, Ty got back in his car and drove around to the garage. He only looked in the rearview mirror three times.

TY WAS AN IDIOT, Marlie thought as she and Ben made their way back to their seats after intermission.

How could he ignore their potential? He'd been stunned; they both had. Last night, Marlie had looked into his eyes and had seen the hot desire and felt the connection that had always been there, waiting for them to acknowledge it. That kiss had certainly acknowledged it; his hands roaming her body had acknowledged it—until Ty remembered he was with Marlie and the connection broke, replaced by shock.

And then came concern and dismay and panic.

Coward. She'd wanted to shake him and tell him to just go with it. And she might have, except she knew all he could see was Marlie with a minivan and a wedding ring. He was totally ignoring all the fun they'd have making kids to put in the minivan.

Speaking of rings... After they sat, she snuggled closer to Ben in the uncomfortable folding chairs inside the Cirque du Soleil tent. Who needed Ty, anyway? He'd slammed the door on their connection, so Marlie would just connect with somebody else.

Like Ben. She'd bet Ben would like to connect. They'd just returned from an interview with Alicia, the reporter, and Ben had stood with his arm around Marlie the entire time. Alicia and her cameraman were still in the tent, talking with the kids down at the front of the stage and the performers who were entertaining them during the break.

Marlie saw the camera pan their way. Ben looked down at her. Oh, why not give Ty something to watch on the news? She smiled an invitation and he accepted immediately. Leaning in, he kissed her softly and then put a little more into it. Good first kiss. Nice. Pleasant. Warm. And totally tingleless.

She was an idiot.

TY LOOKED IN THE FRIDGE and frowned. Marlie must not have had a chance to go grocery shopping. Even the lettuce in the vegetable bin was wilted and slimy.

Ty picked it up to throw it away and discovered an over-flowing trash can beneath the sink—a sink that held his coffee cup and cereal bowl from this morning when he'd used the last of the milk. The empty carton was still on the counter where he'd left it so Marlie would see that they were out of milk.

Ty bagged the trash and took it to the can outside. He opened the lid and was surprised to see last week's trash. Wasn't today garbage pick-up day? Marlie must have forgotten to put out the can.

Back inside, Ty looked around, noticing for the first time that the remotes on the coffee table were exactly where he'd left them the last time he'd watched TV, and not in the caddy. Yesterday's mail was scattered there, too, instead of neatly stacked on the kitchen bar. Just for grins, he slid back the fold-ing doors hiding the washer and dryer. His towels were still in the dryer. Ty did his own laundry, but he never remembered his towels. Marlie would fold them and leave them on top of the dryer, or sometimes even carry them upstairs and leave them on the hall table.

He didn't *ask* her to do it, just as he hadn't asked her to arrange the remotes or gather his mail. And she'd *offered* to grocery shop; he gave her money for his share. If she didn't want to do that anymore, she should have said something.

Would it kill you to get out the mop?

That probably counted as saying something. Ty looked down. The kitchen floor *was* grungy.

He didn't like thinking about kneeling on the kitchen floor with Marlie and kissing her until he forgot where he was. And who he was with. That was the kicker. He shouldn't have forgotten he was kissing Marlie because she was his friend and technically his landlady, as well.

So fine. It *wouldn't* kill him to mop the floor, since she was so busy.

And after mopping the floor, he vacuumed, and straightened the coffee table, and gathered his mail, *and* folded his towels. He even walked a couple of blocks to the convenience store for milk, and on the way back, he picked up the mail from the cluster box, since Marlie hadn't done that, either.

He microwaved the burrito he'd picked up from the store for dinner, checked his email, did a little online Christmas shopping, and sent both sets of his grandparents fruit and cheese baskets.

And then he couldn't stand it any longer and flipped on the TV. He didn't care whether Marlie would be on the news, he told himself. He was just curious to see if the reporter was continuing her series.

He sat through all the commercials and news teasers and didn't hear anything about the date, so he turned off the TV.

He should go to bed and get some extra sleep to make up for last night.

Ty cleared off the coffee table and pointedly replaced the remotes in their stupid caddy.

Then he got the sheets and pillow from the dining table where Marlie had left them instead of hiding them wherever she'd been hiding them. He piled the bedding at the end of the couch instead of making it for her. The stuff was there if she needed it, and if not...

Ty grabbed the remote and clicked on the TV.

"...will it lead to a golden ring?" Alicia Hartson asked from inside the Cirque du Soleil tent. The camera zoomed past her shoulder and focused on a couple making out as acrobats somersaulted through rings and landed on a human pyramid.

Marlie and Ben. Kissing. In front of everyone. In front of Ty. As though to rub it in, the TV station superimposed a pink heart frame around them.

So his plan had worked, Ty told himself. Marlie had found someone. It's what he wanted. And Axelle was going to let the apprentice hostess handle Friday night so she could be with Ty while Marlie was on her colly bird date. He'd wanted that, too. And when he and Axelle were together, he *would* feel a tenth of what he'd felt with Marlie.

Wait—that wasn't what he meant. He meant he'd feel more than he had with Marlie. Then he remembered just how much he'd felt with Marlie and knew he couldn't survive more.

Ty turned off the TV and stared at the blank screen. "Stop thinking about her," he ordered himself out loud.

He should be happy that everything was working out just the way he'd planned. No more worrying about Marlie. He could go to sleep with a clear conscience.

THREE AND A HALF HOURS LATER, Marlie walked upstairs and found Ty eating junk food and watching TV.

"Ty! What are you doing?"

"Clint Eastwood marathon." Crunch. Crunch.

"I didn't realize you were such a fan. Don't you have to get up in, like, four hours?"

He checked his phone for the time and shrugged. The bag crackled as his hand dived back inside.

This was ridiculous. "Did you wait up for me?" Marlie walked around the sofa to confront him.

"Couldn't sleep," he said without looking at her.

She waited, but that seemed to be all he had to say. Leaning forward, he wiped his fingers on a paper towel and held out his hand. "Charm?"

She got the tiny envelope out of her purse and emptied the charm into his palm before sitting next to him.

"It doesn't match." He reached for the pliers he had waiting on the coffee table.

So he *had* stayed up for her—just like a big brother. "It's a gold ring. It shouldn't match." Marlie had never thought of him as a brother and she wasn't about to start now. "Leave a space for the colly bird charm." She took off the bracelet and handed it to him so he could attach the charm without putting her hand on his thigh. It was safer that way.

She gazed at his profile as he opened the jump ring on the charm. Strong jaw. Great mouth. Better before he ate all the onion snacks, though. Maybe that was the point. "We got to meet the performers backstage after the show," Marlie told him to fill the silence. "That's where I've been."

"I'm sure you enjoyed yourself," he said neutrally.

Marlie put a little oomph into her voice. "Oh, I did! It was so much fun! I loved seeing the sets up close and talking to the acrobats. They come from all over the world. And Ben was great. What a clever date idea for five golden rings. You'd think it would be hard to come up with something."

"Not really." Ty handed her the bracelet and picked up the snack bag. He withdrew a handful of crispy yellow onion rings and arranged them on the table in a pyramid. "There. Five golden rings. Done."

"I like Ben's idea better."

"I know. You made the news again." He looked grumpy.

"Alicia says the ratings have been really good, so she plans to keep showing up on the dates."

Ty shifted on the couch and brushed crumbs off the dark, brown fabric. "Does she ask you to do things that will boost the ratings, then?"

Marlie eyed him. "Judging by your thin, disapproving lips, the camera must have caught us kissing." As if she didn't know.

"Yeah."

"That naughty Alicia." Marlie shook her head. "No, the kiss was spontaneous," she said, enjoying telling him. "We'd finished the interview and were talking and, well, you know how it goes." Truthfully, she enjoyed needling Ty more than she'd enjoyed kissing Ben. This was not good.

Ty blew out his breath and reached for an onion ring. "If you like the guy so much, you don't have to go out on the rest of the dates." He didn't meet her eyes.

"I like Ben fine, but we're not going out again." Although she'd had a difficult time convincing Ben. She probably shouldn't have kissed him like that, but she'd been trying to erase the memory of Ty's kiss.

"Why not?" Ty asked.

"He's a high school coach and very athletic. I'm very un-athletic. Besides, he shaves his arms."

Ty snapped his head toward her. "How do you know that?"

"Because the stubble felt scratchy against my tongue when I licked him."

The onion ring crumbled between Ty's fingers.

"Ty, for pity's sake!" Marlie stood, snatched up the snack bag and rolled down the top. She was going to have to air out the place tomorrow. Pointing to her forearm she said, "Here. He shaves this part of his arm. Stop hovering. I swear, my parents didn't wait up and worry as much as you do. Maybe because they trusted my judgment. What a concept."

"I didn't wait up," he insisted. "I couldn't sleep."

Marlie swept the crumbs off the table into her cupped hand and carried them into the kitchen. "You'll be able to get plenty of sleep Friday night. I won't be here. I'm going birding with Jeff Vernon at his family's place near Groveton." She brushed her hands over the sink.

"Where is that?"

"Northeast of Huntsville. I don't know if we'll see any colly birds, but there's a good chance we'll come across a bald eagle."

"You're spending the night?"

Marlie rolled her eyes at the suspicion in his voice. "Yes, Ty. We're going camping. We'll drive up Friday and be back Saturday evening. Now, go to your room. You're in my bed."

"Marlie…"

"I'll leave you all the information." She pointed to the stairs.

Ty stood. "You don't even know this guy."

She smiled. "I will by Saturday."

MR. FOUR COLLY BIRDS, Jeff Vernon, was a good-ole-boy native Texan who worked as a petroleum engineer and loved the outdoors.

Tyler hated him on sight. Or rather he hated him as soon as

Marlie opened the door and the guy gave a low whistle then said, "Why, ain't you the purtiest li'l thang."

Who talked like that?

Then he tilted his cowboy hat and grinned at her as he propped one arm against the door jamb.

Marlie grinned back. Of course she did. Why did women always go for that that "aw shucks, ma'am" stuff?

She stepped aside and he swept off his hat, then wiped his boots on the mat before stepping over the threshold.

"Is this all your gear?" He nodded toward the pile in the entryway.

She'd left a mess of opened boxes and camping equipment beneath the attic access in the upstairs hallway. Ty was going to have to maneuver around it all weekend.

"Yes." Marlie turned and bent to pick up her backpack and sleeping bag.

Jeff angled himself to get a better view and then noticed Ty watching from the top of the stairs. Silently, he pursed his mouth and fanned his hand in a classic, "She's hot" gesture.

Ty now not only hated him, he didn't trust him.

When Marlie straightened, she saw Jeff looking upward and followed his gaze. "That's Ty. He bought the dating package for me."

"Much obliged," Jeff said.

Seriously.

Marlie slung her backpack over her shoulder and Jeff took her sleeping bag. "Thanks for taking off early, Ty."

"No problem."

"My new bed's being delivered this afternoon," she explained to Jeff. "And Ty offered to be here so I wouldn't have to reschedule."

Did she have to say bed? Couldn't she have just said she was waiting for a delivery?

"That's mighty kind of you," Jeff said, and Ty wondered if

the guy had memorized a cowboy phrase book, or if he really talked that way.

"We're fixin' to take off now." Jeff opened the door and ushered Marlie through. "I promise to take real good care of her."

"Did you charge your cell phone, Marlie?" Ty asked pointedly.

"Yes, Ty," she called back in a sing song voice.

"Don't be countin' on that too much," Jeff said. "We've got spotty reception out there. Lots of land and not many people." Jeff met Ty's gaze with a half-smile, winked, and closed the door.

Winked. Ty's blood ran cold.

"TELL ME AGAIN WHY WE ARE here in the woods and not at the symphony?" Axelle shivered and hugged her arms to her body.

Ty struggled to assemble a two-man pup tent—by himself—by lantern light. Maybe if she helped instead of just stood there, she'd generate some body heat. "My family used to go camping all the time," he said. "I thought it would be romantic for us to spend the night under the stars." Within shouting distance of Marlie and Jeff, although if all went well, Axelle would never have to know.

"You can just as easily see the stars from the penthouse of a hotel in Houston," she said. "And there's room service."

"No, you can't." He pounded an orange plastic tent stake into the soft ground. "The city lights make it impossible. Out here, you can see millions of stars."

Axelle looked up. "I see trees." She stamped her feet and rubbed her arms. "I'm so cold! Why is it so much colder out here?"

It wasn't *that* cold, but Ty reminded himself that Axelle

spent her nights around crowds and a steamy kitchen. "We're farther away from the coast. Less humidity, colder nights."

Axelle wasn't dressed for camping. But that was his fault for not giving her any notice before he'd decided that a crisp, clear December night in the woods near Groveton, Texas, was a perfect way to spend time alone with her. She'd done her best with jeans, running shoes and a sweater, but the leather jacket wasn't warm enough for outdoors and Axelle couldn't button it over the bulky sweater.

"Open a sleeping bag and wrap it around yourself," he suggested.

Axelle worked at the knots on one of the bags while he tried to get the tent stakes to hold in the moist ground. Neither succeeded.

"My nails are too long." She dropped the sleeping bag in front of him.

Ty undid the knots in the cord wrapped around the bag.

Axelle unrolled it and made a face. "It stinks!"

"Let it air out," Ty told her. The bags and other equipment dated back to his camping days with Marlie's family. There was a lot to air out. "Hey, give me a hand with this."

Axelle abandoned the sleeping bag in a heap.

"Hold this stake and keep the rope tight," he told her.

She gingerly knelt, grimacing as her knees touched the damp ground. "But why camp now, this very night, instead of when the weather is warmer?"

Ty had a good story prepared. "Men always take you to the symphony, or a play or a lecture or a fabulous restaurant. I wanted to be different. I want our first night together to be memorable."

"And you have succeeded," she said as Ty moved to the opposite corner. "But Tyler, do I appear to be someone who would enjoy sleeping in a tent?"

"You never know until you try." Ty drove in a stake and

looked at her. "It's quiet and peaceful. Nobody to disturb you." He walked back to her, positioned the stake she'd held, and pounded it into the ground. "There. Now hold this."

Axelle gripped a tent pole and Ty fit it to the front of the tent and did the same for the back. A few more stakes and the little orange tent was up.

"How very cozy." Axelle stood and brushed at her knees. "Where are the restrooms?"

"You're kidding."

"No," she said dangerously. "I assume there are public toilets somewhere in the park."

This is where things got tricky. Ty handed her a flashlight. "We're not in a park."

She stared from the flashlight to him. "Where are we?"

"Private property. A guy I know owns the land."

"Would he perhaps live in the house we passed when we turned off the road?"

"Maybe." Ty was surprised she'd noticed, since she'd been complaining about the bumpy ride at the time. "But don't worry. He's probably not home. Nobody will see you."

Her eyes were as wide as any human being's could get.

Ty felt guilty. He did. But not as guilty as he'd feel if Marlie got hurt because some guy decided to take advantage of the fact that they were all alone and no one could hear her call for help.

And, to be honest, he'd hoped Axelle would surprise him and love camping. Until last year, he'd spent a lot of time roughing it outdoors for his job as he walked plots of land and evaluated them for drilling potential.

He missed the outdoors. He wondered if Marlie did.

"You just expect me to…to…" Axelle gestured to the darkness beyond the circle of light cast by the lantern.

"You don't have to go far. I'll stay right by the tent."

Axelle glared at him, muttered something in French, possibly several somethings, and then took off into the darkness.

She was too uptight. A day without modern conveniences would do her good. Ty crawled into the tent and spread out the sleeping bag. Axelle was right. It did stink. So did the tent. He heard her footsteps crunching through the leaves farther and farther away. Keeping his back turned, he unrolled the second sleeping bag and was hit with the aroma of a long-ago campfire. Axelle had mentioned lighting a fire, but Ty didn't want to chance Marlie and Jeff seeing it.

Axelle's annoyance would be nothing like Marlie's fury if she discovered he was spying on her. He wasn't sure where she and Jeff had pitched their tent, but the truck Jeff had been driving when he'd picked up Marlie had been parked by the house, so they had to be within walking distance. Once Axelle went to sleep, Ty would sneak away to see if he could find them.

He stared at the sleeping bags and considered zipping them together. Maybe… He heard Axelle picking her way deeper into the woods and a quick glance over his shoulder showed her light bobbing and getting smaller. No. There would be no reason to zip the bags together.

He exhaled. This would probably be the end of them and, Ty had to admit, he wasn't all that torn up about it. They'd never really seemed to catch fire, not like he and Marlie and that one incredible, unforgettable, sizzler of a kiss which had branded itself in his memory for all time.

For a few moments, he was back in the kitchen, his lips fused with Marlie's, their breaths mingling, their *souls* mingl—

Enough of that. No more mingling.

Ty backed out of the tent and hung his backpack in a tree out of the way of any animals wandering by. He glanced toward the direction Axelle had gone, but couldn't see her flashlight beam. He couldn't hear her, either.

Great. He should have given her the flashlight with the fresh batteries. Grabbing it now, he took off after her. Seconds later, he saw her light, still bobbing as she walked.

"Axelle!"

No response.

Ty jogged after her. "Axelle!" She had to have heard him crashing through the woods, but she didn't stop until he tagged her arm.

She whipped around and snarled at him. "What?"

"Where are you going?"

"To the house." She pointed through the trees. "I can see light from the windows, so I am going to knock on the door and ask to use the toilet."

Ty gripped her arm. "That's not a good idea."

"Why not? Why can I not go to the house? Surely your 'friend' is aware that we are camping on his property?"

Ty thought fast. "Just because someone is at the house doesn't mean *he's* there. It could be anyone, maybe even somebody who's not supposed to be there."

"Speakin' of which," drawled a deep voice as an intense beam of light suddenly blinded him. "You're trespassing."

Axelle screamed in Ty's ear, making it ring. "He's got a gun!"

11

"TY?" MARLIE STARED AT the two people squinting against Jeff's spotlight. Unbelievable. Ty and Axelle. *Axelle.* Bizarre enough for Ty to be there, but with Axelle?

"Hi, Marlie." He held up a hand to shade his eyes.

Jeff moved the beam out of his face. "Axelle, hon, is that you?"

"Jeffrey?" She exhaled and pressed her palm to her chest.

"The one and only." He lowered the gun. "What're y'all doin' here?"

Oh, good question. *Excellent* question. Marlie would like to hear the answer to that question.

"Trying to find a toilet," Axelle said with dignity.

"Well, come on to the house and we'll get you fixed up." Jeff glanced at Marlie.

"Go on ahead," she told him. "Ty and I will catch up."

Jeff nodded, and then he and Axelle moved off, Axelle talking rapidly, and not always in English.

Marlie stared at Ty. "I don't believe this. I do *not* believe you followed us."

"At least I waited until your bed was delivered." He flashed one of his charming Ty smiles at her. "Looks good."

She was not charmed. She couldn't believe he was trying to be funny about the situation, either. "I don't know which is more incredible—that you actually drove all the way here, or that you brought Axelle with you."

"It wasn't that far—just a couple of hours, and I thought she might enjoy herself" he had the nerve to say.

"Enjoy what? Camping? Or spying on me and Jeff? Are you guys into voyeurism?"

"Come on, Marlie." He took a step toward her, looking irritated when she backed away. "I had a bad feeling about this whole set-up."

"Why?"

"You didn't see the way he looked at you." Ty's jaw tightened. "He winked at me, Marlie."

She was flabbergasted. "Winked?"

"Yeah." Ty nodded and shifted his weight. "Guys don't wink at other guys."

"And Axelle agreed that winking indicates Jeff is seriously deranged?" She saw Ty's face. "You didn't *tell* her we were here?"

"I'd hoped it wouldn't be necessary."

"I'll bet you did. You've got a fun conversation ahead of you."

"I know," he muttered.

"What were you planning to do, anyway, Ty? Hide in the bushes and jump out if Jeff tried to kiss me?"

"If I had to!" He swung his hand, his flashlight beam arcing across the trees. "'Cause I sure don't see anybody else out here to rescue you if you get into trouble."

"And by trouble, you mean sex. Because I'm so obviously distraught over not having sex with you, that I'll just run out and have sex with anybody!" Marlie had a sudden urge to either strangle him or tear her hair out. She crossed her arms over her chest just in case.

He looked off to the side, jaw working, then back at her. "What was I to think? The very next day after we…" He gestured, which made her even angrier.

"Had our moment?" She bit off the "*t*."

"Yes. Just hours after that, you were kissing Bob—"

"Ben."

"—on TV!"

"Your point?"

"That *was* my point!"

"It's a stupid point! You said forget it. I forgot it." Marlie turned and headed back to the house. She heard Ty crunching through the leaves and pine needles behind her. If he were anybody but Ty, she'd say he was jealous.

"Marlie." He touched her arm.

"Leave me alone!"

"No. I'm concerned about you."

She whirled around. "Why?"

He stopped short. "Because…"

And for a moment, Marlie thought—*hoped*—Ty would say it was because he couldn't stop thinking about her and the thought of her with another man was killing him since he'd realized he was madly in love with her.

They stood close enough for Marlie to see the starlight reflected in his eyes. Close enough to fall into each other's arms. She wished they would because she was just so tired of trying not to be in love with him. "Because?" she prompted, softly.

"Because you're all alone out here with that guy. No cell reception, Marlie."

So much for a declaration of everlasting love. "Oooo. We're *aaaallll aloooone*," she said, wiggling her hands. "That is, if you don't count Jeff's parents, his sister and brother-in-law, and five Cub Scouts."

Ty blinked. "What are you talking about?"

"Listen." In the distance, high-pitched, childish voices shrieked and laughed. "Jeff's sister is a Cub Scout leader and this is their first campout," she told him. "She needed more adults to spend the night, so Jeff asked if I minded coming up a day early and filling in for one of the parents who couldn't be here. I said sure."

Ty drew a breath. "I didn't know."

"You didn't ask."

"Why would I think to ask if there'd be Cub Scouts on your date?" he snapped.

"Why do you care?"

"Because I bought these dates, so I feel responsible for your safety."

Responsibility is all he'll ever feel for you. "We're not kids anymore. I'm responsible for my own safety. Anyway, as you saw, Jeff's got it covered."

Ty made a noise. "And *that's* supposed to make me feel better about him?"

"It doesn't?"

"He had a gun, Marlie," Ty said in a low voice. "Around kids."

"It was locked in his truck until you and Axelle scared us."

"And then he takes *you* to check us out instead of another man? We could have been anybody."

Was Ty aware of how irrational he sounded? She spoke slowly and very deliberately. "The other man was helping his wife herd Cub Scouts into the house where Jeff's dad was getting a shotgun out of the *locked gun cabinet* so he could come help."

Ty's response to that was to stare at her while breathing deeply. The crisp, cool air carried the sound of the boys' excited chatter laced with adult murmurings. Marlie could smell the smoke from the campfire inside the ring of rocks the boys had collected and arranged.

She and Ty used to have that job when they'd camped, so, of course, that had made her think of him when she didn't want to think of him. And now, here he was, intruding on her thoughts in person.

Ironically, he was wrecking her love life after all those years of complaining that she was ruining his. If he didn't want a future with her, then he needed to go away. Completely. None of this concerned, platonic caring, emphasis on the platonic. No more.

"So have I explained everything?" she asked. "Allayed all your fears? Before you answer, consider that mothers have trusted their seven-year-olds to this family."

"I get it." He nodded tightly. "I misjudged the situation." His flashlight dimmed and he struck it against his thigh making it bright again. "But I meant well, and you're not even the slightest bit grateful. I could have been at the symphony right now—and those tickets weren't cheap—instead of standing in the woods getting yelled at."

How was that her fault? "And I could be getting to know a man who seems to be a really great guy. Right now, he and his family are probably wondering what's wrong with me, since my stalker friend doesn't trust my judgment."

Just then, there was a sudden, loud monster voice from the direction of the campfire, followed by screams that dissolved into laughter and hooting. "I should get back," she said.

"I'm sorry I ruined your date." Ty sounded a lot like a kid being forced to say he was sorry, something Marlie had heard a couple of times just this evening.

"Are you kidding? The night's just getting started. We're cooking s'mores and telling ghost stories around the fire.

However you—" she poked him in the chest "—are not invited. Go home, Ty. Get your stuff and I'll tell Axelle you'll pick her up at the house."

IT WAS AFTER MIDNIGHT WHEN Ty pulled in front of the loft Axelle shared with Paul. It had been an ominously quiet two hours. Although Axelle had kept her eyes closed the entire time, as the car slowed she sat up and Ty guessed she hadn't been asleep. Just avoiding talking with him.

Could he blame her? "I'm sorry for dragging you out there with me," he began. "I was concerned—"

She cut him off. "I accept your apology. We do not need to discuss this further." She reached for the door handle.

There was no way she was going to just drop the subject. "I'll call you."

"Please don't." She sat motionless, her hand on the door handle before releasing it and easing back in the seat. Then she turned to look straight at him. "You're in love with Marlie."

"What? No," he denied automatically. "She's a friend. I care what happens to her, that's all. It's habit."

"That is not all." She gave him a disgusted look and said something in French. "I thought it would be amusing to watch you come to realize you loved her. Maybe even nudge you here and there. And Paul!" She rolled her eyes. "I told him he was being too heavy-handed in trying to make you jealous, and now I must apologize to him because, clearly, he was not heavy-handed enough!"

"Paul was trying to make me jealous?" Ty replayed a few memorable moments from that night. He'd been concerned that Marlie wouldn't recognize Paul's insincerity. Even now, the thought of her in Paul's insincere French arms made Ty's stomach knot, made his blood heat, made him want to punch the guy—

Made him jealous. Teeth-grittingly jealous. Made him want

Marlie in *his* arms and nobody else's. The shock of it made Ty's heart pound. This was bad. He was way too involved. He needed to back off and fast. How could Marlie move on if Ty stood in her way? "But…I was with you. You're his sister. Why would Paul want me to be jealous?"

Axelle flung up her hands. "This is why you are not fun for me anymore. You refuse to see what is in front of you." She eyed him. "Leave her alone. She does not need you or your 'concern'."

"Oh, I got the memo. You bet I'm going to leave Marlie alone." He'd find one of those hotels that rented furnished studio apartments by the week and stay far, far away from Marlie. Let her find someone who wanted to carpool kids and mow lawns and…and lead Cub Scouts. Ty wanted to travel and eat in expensive restaurants and not worry about sticky fingerprints on white sofas. He and Marlie'd go back to hearing about each other during phone calls with their moms. They'd never have to see each other again.

His life would be perfect—except that Marlie wouldn't be in it.

At the thought of a life without Marlie, a sense of profound desolation washed through him, scrubbing away all the lies he'd told himself to cover up the truth.

And, undeniably, the truth was that he *was* in love with her.

He was in love with Marlie. Love love. With *Marlie.*

No. Not Marlie.

Yes, Marlie.

As soon as he quit fighting the idea, a tension he'd been living with for as long as he could remember eased, to be replaced by yearning. He yearned for *her. Yearned.* For the first time, deep emotions fueled his physical desire. His entire adult life he'd had it backward. He'd used sex to try to find an emotional connection. With Marlie, he had the emotional connection and his body wanted to celebrate physically. And celebrate often.

He gripped the steering wheel to calm the trembling in his hands as waves of intense feeling crashed through him. All his ideas about the kind of life he wanted collapsed and disappeared like the scenery between acts of a play. The curtain was ready to go up on the next act and there was Marlie, not on the empty stage, not waiting in the wings for her cue, but out in the audience, watching him.

Probably sitting next to Axelle and the other women he'd auditioned and rejected. Only Marlie had got the part and didn't know it. Ty hadn't even known it until just now.

But maybe she was no longer interested. He glanced at Axelle, who'd gone quiet. "Does… Do you think Marlie loves me?"

Axelle gave him a pity-filled look and shrugged. "It does not matter whether or not Marlie loves you if you don't *want* her love. You are too tame for her, anyway."

"Tame?"

"You think too much," Axelle said. "Marlie is passionate like me."

"Marlie? Passionate?" And then he remembered how she'd come alive in his arms, which sent another wave of heat through him.

"Yes!" Axelle leaned forward, getting right in his face. "She loves with her whole heart!" She punctuated the words with a fist to her chest. "I understood this about her the night you told me the way her fiancé left her. He stomped her heart into little bitty pieces and then threw them back at her! It takes a woman a *very* long time to put her heart back together after such as that." Axelle straightened, her disappointed eyes gazing into his. "Marlie is wise to guard her heart. Why should she give it to someone who doesn't want it?"

"What if I do want it?" he retorted.

"What if?" Axelle erupted. *"What if?"*

Ty leaned away from her outrage.

"How will you decide? Borrow her heart and try it out like a car? Sign a lease in case you change your mind? Use it and give it back a little worse for the wear?"

"No!" Ty looked into Axelle's angry face and realized that while he'd been having life-changing epiphanies, the last thing he'd said to Marlie had been that he was going to leave her alone. "I—"

"Why do you think it is all your decision, anyway? Maybe Marlie doesn't want *your* heart."

Cold panic gripped him and he realized another truth, one that was both unnerving and exhilarating. "It doesn't matter whether she wants it or not. She's already got it." His lips twisted. "You're right. I love her."

Axelle's face transformed, softened. "At last you admit it," she whispered. "Thank you."

Ty felt very calm for a man who had just told the woman he was with that he was in love with another. Axelle was looking at him with an amused tenderness. Yeah, this was really funny. The woman he loved was mad at him and he'd finally clicked with the woman he'd rejected. "How long have you—"

"—have I known you loved her?" Axelle laughed lightly. "Since the night you told me how her fiancé left her. I said to myself, 'He loves her and he doesn't know. This could be very amusing, especially if she feels the same way.' And I wanted to see that moment of realization between the two of you. I wanted to see the love catch hold and grow."

Ty was totally baffled. It must be a French thing. "Why?"

"To remember." Axelle looked away. "To remind myself that such a thing as true love exists."

And she'd known it once, Ty sensed with the clarity of one newly in love. He touched her shoulder. "Someone hurt you?"

Shaking her head, Axelle opened the door, and he thought she'd leave without answering. "I'm a widow," she whispered before slamming the door and hurrying into the building.

A widow. Ty sat in the car for a long time. Long enough to see her standing, head bowed, waiting for the elevator. Long enough to see her step inside. So much about Axelle's reserve made sense now. Life had "stomped her heart into little, bitty pieces."

If Marlie stomped his heart to bits and threw it back at him, he'd glue it together and give it to her again. Ty lowered his head to the steering wheel. That sentiment, if nothing else, told him he loved her. If it hadn't been for Axelle and Paul, he might not have figured it out until it was too late.

It might already be too late. Even so, he owed Axelle a debt that could never be repaid. Paul? Not so much. He didn't owe Paul anything.

Ty started the car and pulled away from the curb. He wanted to race home to Marlie, except Marlie wasn't there. She was spending the night with the virile Jeff, who was using Cub Scouts to make himself look oh-so-attractive. Women loved men who worked with kids. Women also loved men who cooked for them, and made them laugh, and knew their way around a wine list.

And men whose sizzling kisses took their breath away.

But not the incredibly stupid ones who told them the kisses meant nothing and left them half-naked on the kitchen floor. No. Women didn't like that.

Ty came to a stop and gazed unseeingly across the intersection at cars driving in and out of a lot strung with lights. Overhead, a sign blinked: 24-hour Xmas trees!

He had to get Marlie back. Except, he'd never really had her to begin with, and now he was not only competing against the dozen men he'd surrounded her with, but he'd already rejected her in a big way. Marlie had his heart, but didn't know it. Even if she did, there was no guarantee she'd want it.

Ty had a lot to overcome, but he had a couple of advantages: he lived with her and they had incredible chemistry. If she'd forgotten, as she claimed—because he'd stupidly told her to—then he would remind her. As often as necessary.

But that wouldn't be enough because she wouldn't trust his motives, not after he'd repeatedly insisted they wanted totally different lives. To be honest, he wasn't ready to buy into the whole domestic bliss in suburbia package—just the part that included Marlie. The bliss part. For now. A grin stole across his face as he imagined a couple of little Marlies running around, bushy ponytails bobbing.

Then he groaned and closed his eyes. He *did* want the whole package. When did that happen? *How* did that happen? He was sickeningly in love, that's how it happened. But how was he going to convince Marlie when he could barely believe it himself?

Behind him, a car horn beeped, alerting him that the light had turned green. Driving through the intersection, Ty had to wait next to the blinking sign as cars with Christmas trees tied on top gingerly turned onto the street.

And a thought blinked into his head. With Marlie, it wasn't the going out, it was the staying in. That was the key. Woo her on the domestic front and the bliss would follow. Make love to her house before making love to her. Show her he wanted the same life she did. He'd have to embrace his inner homemaker as he laid the domestic groundwork, but the payoff would be bliss.

Such a strategy would require patience, commitment, and, Ty clicked on his turn signal, a Christmas tree.

12

LATE SATURDAY AFTERNOON, Marlie said goodbye to Jeff, a nice, handsome, responsible, kid-loving man who wanted a family of his own—but for whom Marlie felt no enthusiasm about the activity necessary to produce said family—opened her front door, and walked into a wall of pine needles. She couldn't get inside her townhouse and close her front door at the same time. In fact, now that she'd opened the front door, the branches had sprung out and she couldn't close it at all.

"Ty?" she called to the man for whom she felt wild enthusiasm at the thought of the act that would produce a family. Too bad she couldn't produce children with him and raise them with Jeff. Nice as Jeff was, she didn't think he'd go for the idea. And as irritating as Ty was, he wouldn't either.

"Hey, you're back!" she heard him say. He sounded very cheery for someone who should be skulking around with his tail between his legs. "I can use the help."

Understatement. "What did you do, bring home a souvenir from your little jaunt in the woods?"

"Are you still mad about that?"

"Yes!" Actually, she was over it, but he didn't need to know. Jeff had thought Ty sneaking around the woods to check up on her was funny, and he was truly impressed that Ty had managed to get Axelle out there with him.

"Do you think you could stop being mad long enough to push from your end so we can get the tree upstairs?" he asked.

Marlie couldn't even see upstairs. The tree filled the entire staircase. "It's too big!"

"No, the stairway is too small." The branches quivered as Ty grabbed the other end. "Let me make sure I've got the stand on real tight."

"I thought I was supposed to buy the Christmas tree."

"You've been too busy. By the time you'd have gotten around to it, all the good ones would have been taken."

Marlie smiled and shook her head. "You think buying a Christmas tree will make me stop being angry that you embarrassed me?"

"Yes, because you're going to be angry about what the branches are doing to your walls."

Marlie stepped sideways and brushed the tips away from the wall revealing dirty scratches. "Ty!"

"I'll repaint. Okay, ready?"

Marlie stuck her hand into the branches at the top of the tree. As she felt around for a good grip, needles dropped to the foyer tile. She could only imagine what the carpet on the stairs was going to look like when this was finished. "You'll have to vacuum, too."

"I know. Push."

Marlie pushed, wincing as the branches scraped and left brown and green marks on the off-white paint. She, herself, ended up more scratched than she'd been after a day tromping through the woods.

At last, she and Ty wrestled the tree into the spot he'd prepared in front of the bay window. Prepared, as in shoving everything out of the way. He had a ladder waiting, and using a rope and Marlie's help, he maneuvered the tree upright.

It jounced into place, teetered, and settled, branches rippling, needles dropping, a monster tree that blocked most of the light from the window and extended so far into the room that Ty had had to move the furniture.

"How tall is it?" she asked.

"Seventeen feet. Isn't it a beauty?" He fisted his hands at his waist, feet apart, and admired his tree as though he'd cut it down himself.

"It's really something."

"It wouldn't fit on my car, so I paid a couple of the high-school kids who worked at the lot to bring the tree by in their truck," he told her. "They would have helped me get it up here, but I needed to buy a bigger stand. This baby is going to suck up some serious water."

Why wasn't she angry with him? Why was she feeling, oh, *charmed* that he'd bought a giant tree for just the two of them? "You're crazy."

A corner of his mouth went up. "A little."

"A lot. How are we going to get it out of here after the holidays? The branches will be dry and stiff and they'll leave gouges that'll take more than paint to fix."

"I'll chop it into pieces first."

"You're planning on bringing a chainsaw into the living room?"

"Can I?" He grinned and Marlie steeled herself against it. And him.

"No."

They stared at the tree in silence. Marlie was trying not to think that this was the first and only Christmas they'd have together and she was also trying not to think how irritatingly good Ty looked in an ancient paint-spattered sweatshirt with the sleeves ripped off. She wished she could stay angry with him. It would be easier.

"Axelle broke up with me," Ty said.

Like that was a surprise. "I'm sorry."

"I'm not. She wasn't my type."

"She was exactly your type."

"My type has changed," he said. "Now my type has to like camping."

Marlie sucked air through her teeth. "I don't know. Perfectly groomed women in designer clothes and shoes aren't the 'get-close-to-nature' types. They're working hard to get *away* from nature. And the campers don't want to bother with hair and makeup and nails. They'd rather have a good pair of hiking boots than a strappy sandal that shows off their pedicure."

He met her eyes. "Then I guess I'm looking for a babe in the woods."

"Ha. Good luck with that." She remembered him telling her she was a babe. He had to remember it, too. But that was when her hair wasn't bunched up in a pony tail and she was wearing makeup and a sexy dress and hadn't just spent a day and night camping with a bunch of Cub Scouts.

He gazed steadily at her. "What are you looking for?"

He already knew. Did he think she'd changed? Did he hope she'd changed? "My usual. Someone who wants to be with me for better or worse, for richer or poorer, in sickness and health, from two a.m. feedings to graduation. Someone who'll be there for me rain or shine." And she could not be clearer than that.

Her heart wished Ty'd be that man, but her heart was on probation after Eric.

"You left out something," he said.

"I thought that pretty much covered it."

"Passion."

He was right. Had she left out passion because she instinctively knew she wouldn't find it with anyone but Ty? Her heart started pounding so hard she felt the blood pulsing in her ears. *Stop it.* Ty had told her to forget passion with him and she couldn't, so she was trying to find passion with someone else. So far, she couldn't do that, either. It wasn't fair!

"Marlie," he said, his voice deep and his eyes hot.

That wasn't fair, either. When he looked at her like that and said her name all raggedy, she wanted to kiss him, in spite of knowing his kisses would make her change her type from year-round to seasonal.

She backed away. "I need to shower and change. Mr. Six Geese a Laying is taking me to a comedy club for a performance of 'Goosed'."

"Tonight?" Ty looked disappointed. And hot. Always hot.

Marlie kept backing out of the room. "It is Saturday night."

"Oh. Right." He turned to the window. "I'd kinda thought we'd decorate the tree together."

"I don't have any ornaments."

"You don't?" He sounded surprised.

"I just had a couple of strings of lights and some cheapie balls. I tossed them before we moved."

"So this is your first Christmas tree here?" he asked.

She nodded and headed for the stairs to her bedroom.

"Then we'll have to go all out," he said with ominous cheer.

"Ty, there's a seventeen-foot tree in my living room. We've already gone all out."

"Oh—Marlie?" he called as she reached the bottom steps. "I set up your bed and...other stuff." He shoved his hands into the pockets of his jeans. "I hope it's okay."

"The bed!" She let her head fall back. "I'd forgotten all

about it." And now she was going to have to make the thing and maybe move it around and she was *so tired.* "Thanks."

Her backpack and sleeping bag were still downstairs, but Marlie wanted to check out the new bed. The hallway outside her room smelled different, like packing material and fabric dye and…fresh paint? She pressed the light switch and gasped softly.

The bed was in exactly the right spot, allowing her to see out the window when she woke up. Ty had already made it up with the new bedding she'd bought—the sand colored sheets and duvet and decorative pillows in bleached blues and greens. And then he'd painted the walls in the palest sea-glass-green.

Marlie felt instantly soothed, wrapped in serenity. Lighter than she'd ever, ever felt when she walked into her bedroom. She could breathe in here again.

The backs of her eyes burned when she thought of all the months the other bed had battered her spirit. Ty had understood that, and more. He'd known exactly what she needed and when she'd shopped for linens, she'd been drawn to the colors and fabric he'd described.

Marlie sat on the bed and held the outrageously expensive pillow she'd used for inspiration. It was decorated with a sea glass mosaic, and she'd bought the bedding to match, never intending to buy the pillow, too—paying over two hundred dollars for a pillow was stupid. But it made her happy to look at it, so she bought it, anyway, because sometimes the heart wants what the heart wants.

She touched one of the smooth pieces of pale, cloudy green-blue glass on the pillow. Ty had guessed that it was her favorite and then painted her walls with the color.

As an apology, it was pretty spectacular.

Marlie started leaking tears from her eyes. Not actively crying, but not fighting it, either.

Eric had never done anything like this for her. He wouldn't have known how. Nobody had ever done anything like this for her. Nobody but Ty.

Marlie set the pillow back before tears dropped on it. Wiping her cheeks, she walked out into the hallway to the top of the stairs.

Ty stood at the bottom.

Sometimes the heart wants what the heart wants. But sometimes the heart can't have what it wants.

They looked at each other for long moments before Marlie said, "Okay, you're forgiven. For all of it. You've got a clean slate. Don't blow it."

YES! HE WAS IN. BARELY. He'd nearly lost his mind when he'd mentioned she'd forgotten about passion, and then watched her face as she remembered it. Her lips had parted and her face had flushed and her eyes had gone dreamy and he'd been seconds away from kissing her.

Ty shook his head to clear away the image. He had a strategy in place and he was determined to stick to it. Lay groundwork and have patience.

Therefore, he was on his best behavior when the goose guy arrived to pick up Marlie. And when she got home, he didn't have to pretend to be engrossed in the TV because he was still painting the stairway walls. Before breaking out the leftover builder's paint he'd found in the garage, it had taken him forever to suck up all the pine needles. Or most of them. He suspected he'd burned up the vacuum cleaner motor. It sure smelled like it.

So when the front door opened, he had a legitimate reason for being a few feet away, for lifting a hand to the goose guy, who smiled, and told Marlie good-night—without kissing her.

She shut the door.

"Have a good time?" he asked, oh-so-very casually.

"Yeah." She stood and watched him. "It was kind of a wacky 'Christmas Carol' type show."

"Sounds like fun." Did she notice how he wasn't asking about the goose guy? Did she?

"Matt's getting married," Marlie said, as though he'd asked. "He got engaged after he told Axelle he'd participate in the auction."

Matt was the goose guy, which meant six down, six to go. "It was nice of him not to back out. Good man." He could be generous when nothing was at stake.

Ty scanned the wall for areas that needed another coat of paint. "Did I miss any places?"

"Behind you," Marlie said.

Ty turned around and dabbed at a spot where the green was still visible. "The sap or something is bleeding through the paint."

"It'll be okay. Who knows? I like my bedroom so much I might want to repaint the whole place in something besides builder's white."

He smiled down at her. "I like color."

She smiled up at him. "So do I."

Her face was open and friendly and pretty and they were standing close enough together that Ty was getting a little dizzy with the effort it took not to bend down a few inches and kiss her.

Now was not the time. Now was the time for him to romance all things domestic. But sticking to his strategy was going to be impossible if she kept looking at him as though she was thinking about that one, incredible, hot, life-changing session in the kitchen.

Fortunately, paint dripped from the brush onto his hand before he could add an incredible, hot, life-changing kiss on the stairs to their memories. Later. They'd make memories later. Lots of memories so she'd never again list everything she wanted in life and leave out passion.

Ty grabbed for a rag as Marlie stepped by him.

"You'll be pleased to know I have a golden egg for my charm, so the ring won't be the only gold on the bracelet."

He nodded and concentrated on wiping the paint off his hand and the brush handle and not looking at her. "Leave it on the kitchen counter with the bird charm, and I'll attach them when I finish up here."

"Okay. Thanks, Ty. And for my room, too. I can hardly wait to sleep in it."

Me, too, he thought. Then he broke down and watched her run up the stairs and second-guessed himself. If the chemistry had been that great before he knew he loved her, how great would it be between them now?

Stick to the plan. Patience and groundwork. Not only did he have to demonstrate domestic commitment, he had to look as though he enjoyed it. Which, oddly, he did. Go figure.

So Ty stared at paint drying until he was absolutely certain he could walk past Marlie's bedroom without trying to join her in her brand-new, big, soft, comfortable bed.

THE NEXT DAY, MARLIE WENT to a synchronized swimming competition and ate dinner at the Black Swan Pub with Mr. Seven Swans a Swimming.

Ty patiently attached a silver swan charm to her bracelet and saw Marlie watching little girls in weird glittery makeup form flower patterns with their legs in the water on the ten o'clock news.

On Monday, Ty bought a new vacuum cleaner and Marlie milked a cow on the ten-o'clock news. After patiently attaching a cow charm to the bracelet, he shared the cheese and crackers she'd brought home with her, right there in the living room next to the naked Christmas tree.

Marlie had said nothing about the tree since informing him she had no ornaments. They were supposed to decorate the tree together, damn it. Shared domesticity. Sentimentality. Sappy Christmas music. Hot chocolate. Cookies. Groundwork. But she had to *want* to decorate the tree and so far, she'd ignored the thing, although how was a mystery.

Patience. Remember the bliss, he told himself.

Having patience meant that on Tuesday, Ty watched clips of Marlie in the arms of another man on the ten o'clock news as she took dance lessons with the second Jason, Mr. Nine Ladies Dancing. She still wasn't home and that was because Alicia Hartson was broadcasting live as nine ladies—eight plus Marlie—belly danced.

Belly. Danced.

And he'd thought watching her with another man had been difficult. Now, he, and any other man watching, saw Marlie's hips swiveling and shaking. She was surprisingly limber. Ty stared, mesmerized, and thought of those hips under him. On top of him. Surrounding a very specific part of his anatomy. He thought of Marlie's face, soft with passion, and her hair brushing creamy shoulders and the soft skin he remembered. His fingertips tingled, eager to explore more of the skin.

He needed a faster plan.

WEDNESDAY NIGHT FOUND Marlie in the kitchen heating up a festival of saturated fat.

Ty stood at the top of the stairs and sniffed. "I smell wonderful things."

"Yeah, a billion calories of fat, salt, bread and cheese," she said.

"Nectar of the gods."

"Fat gods." Marlie bent to look in the oven window. "Randy—you remember him from the auction?" She looked over her shoulder at him.

Ty was instantly transported to the last time Marlie was in the kitchen looking at him from that position. He'd stupidly messed up by telling himself she wasn't the right woman for him when she'd always been the right woman for him. It had only taken years and years and years for him to figure it out. What if he went into the kitchen right now and they pretended the last week had never happened? Just continued from the point where she had reached for his belt and he'd stopped her. Only this time he wouldn't stop her. They could—the floor was clean now.

He was going to use *the floor is clean now* as a romantic come-on? Charming. *Stay out of the kitchen,* Ty told himself. He gripped the handles of the shopping bags he carried as he managed to nod, that, yes, he remembered Randy.

She turned back to the oven. "He's Ten Lords a Leaping. He brought over frozen potato skins, fried cheese, boneless buffalo wings, jalapeño cheese poppers and pizza rolls."

"I like Randy." Ty carried red and white shopping bags over to their tree, carefully positioning them so the Santa's North Pole Outlet logo was visible.

"Good, because he's downstairs in my office setting up for our date." Marlie plopped a roll of paper towels on a tray.

"Which is?"

The buzzer sounded on the oven. "We're networking our computers to play Dominion of Zartha online."

Ty blinked.

Marlie slipped her hand into an oven mitt. "He's formed a guild called the Ten Leaping Lords and we're going on a raid to try and capture Finraz, Chancellor of Quarol. Isn't that clever of him?"

"I don't know. If I translated correctly, you just told me you're going to stay here and play online computer games?"

"Exactly." She removed the tray from the oven.

Ty snorted. "Cheap date."

"Shh. Give him a break. He's only twenty-three." She held up her arm with the charm bracelet. "He already gave me the charm."

Ty walked over to take a look. "It's a letter 'Z'."

Marlie nodded. "For Zartha."

"It's made out of a paper clip."

"Maybe." Marlie picked up the tray and nodded toward a two-liter bottle of soda.

Shaking his head, Ty picked it up, along with two glasses filled with ice, and followed her downstairs.

Ty made two more trips out to his car and heard laughter each time he passed by her office. He looked in and saw them wearing head phones and typing madly away.

And what was he doing? Wrapping lights on the tree. Colored lights because they both liked color. Thousands of colored lights. Many, many strings of lights requiring extension cords and outlet strips.

And patience.

There was no bliss.

Later, when he was finished and Marlie and Randy were still slaying dragons or whatever they were doing, Ty turned out all the room lights, leaving the Christmas tree lit.

There was something magical about a lighted Christmas tree in a dark room. He only hoped the magic would work on Marlie.

FAR, FAR TOO MANY HOURS later, Marlie said goodbye to Randy and his computer and carried the tray with their dirty dishes upstairs. On her way up, she saw the rainbow glow coming from the living room and knew what it meant, but she wasn't prepared for the breathtaking spectacle of a fully-lit, seventeen-foot Christmas tree.

She looked around the room, but didn't see Ty. Setting her

tray on the kitchen bar, Marlie sat on the couch and hugged her knees to her chest.

It must have taken him hours to wrap the tree in lights. Just for the two of them. Just because he wanted to celebrate Christmas with her. That had to mean something. But what?

Briefly, she allowed herself to remember the hot look in his eyes, the one that could melt her resolve to stop wanting him That Way.

What are you looking for? he'd asked her.

Like a dummy, she'd mentioned everything but passion. She could tell he wanted to give her a little friendly reminder to add it to her list because clearly it had been so long since she'd had any, she'd forgotten how important it was.

She hadn't forgotten. But she'd been burned the last time she'd followed her heart, so this time, she was following her mind. Commitment, or the possibility first, passion second, no matter how much her heart pouted.

The only reason she was looking good to Ty right now was because he was between girlfriends. As soon as a sleek, designer-clad, Pilates-toned woman caught his eye, he'd be gone. He'd be moving out soon, anyway. Out of sight, out of mind, as they say.

From nowhere, the thought of living here without Ty walloped her, and she burst into tears, shocking herself. Her mind was telling her that she'd known this was coming, but her heart was throwing a fit. Marlie clapped both hands over her mouth in an effort to stifle her sobs, amazed at their depth. She hadn't cried this hard over Eric. Over anything. Ever.

The colored lights of the tree smeared together. It was late and she was tired and where did she have to go? Into the bedroom Ty had painted for her.

She loved that bedroom and now she was going to have

to redecorate or she'd think about him every time she was in it.

How dare he ruin her bedroom for her? She'd barely had time to enjoy it. Gulping back her sobs, she wiped her eyes, dried her fingers on her jeans, and then yanked out the cord to the lights on the Christmas tree.

13

MARLIE'S DIZZYING SOCIAL whirl had severely cut into her work time. No work meant no money and so far, December had been an expensive month with the new clothes and shoes and hair maintenance and, wow, underwear sure cost a lot these days. She hadn't even gone Christmas shopping yet. Fortunately, she had a couple of days before her piper and drummer dates. They were both going to be this weekend at the Houston Highland Games, the piper on Saturday and the drummer on Sunday.

Marlie got to work updating websites for clients running after-Christmas sales and designing mock-ups for the new clients she'd acquired as a result of her work on the auction website. She barely noticed the passing hours until Ty walked by her office.

He was carrying grocery-store bags. "Have you eaten yet?"

"No." She gave him an apologetic look. "I keep meaning to go to the store."

"No prob. I'm making us salads. I'll call you when they're ready."

Marlie stared after him, analyzing what he'd just said. Ty was fixing a meal. For both of them. Salads. Salads? Did that count as cooking for her? If so, why? And he'd been picking up the household chores she'd let slide, too, not to mention the tree. No. She wouldn't mention the tree. He was being thoughtful and considerate. This was not normal for him. How could they go back to normal if he kept acting nice to her?

Marlie couldn't concentrate, so she gave up and climbed the stairs.

Ty had actually set the table with placemats and everything. "Hey, I was just about to call you."

"I got to a stopping place." This was all very nice and homey. He must want something.

He set two plates of salad on the table and gestured. "Take a seat."

Marlie sat and noticed that she was facing the lit Christmas tree. Behind her, Ty turned out the kitchen light leaving the tree as the sole source of illumination. And it was plenty.

Okay, what was up? "So, Ty. Salad?"

He flashed her a smile as he slipped into the chair at the end of the table, leaving her a clear view of the tree. "After last night's junk food orgy, you need veggies."

"True," Marlie agreed, and speared a forkful of lettuce. After chewing and swallowing, she mixed up the greens before taking another bite. "Ty? Is there dressing on the salad?"

"No," he said. "I put in a few pieces of grilled chicken from the deli and a couple of those yellow peppers you like. Some carrots, too. Nothing to interfere with the flavor of the lettuce."

Apparently, he was serious. Not wanting to criticize him and discourage him from ever "cooking" for her again, Marlie ate another couple of bites before giving in. "I think I'd prefer just a little dressing." She went to the fridge, brought out an assortment of individual packets left over from previous take-out meals, and dropped them in a pile on the table. After sorting through them, she picked a low-cal vinaigrette and dribbled it on her salad. "Ah. Much better."

Ty watched her eat, and then chose one for himself. "You're right. It is better with dressing."

Marlie narrowed her eyes, but said nothing.

He smiled. "That's true for a lot of things."

"What's true?"

"Oh...sometimes things need a little boost. A little extra."

"What things?" she asked suspiciously.

"Well, mashed potatoes need gravy. Pancakes need syrup." He looked around. "Walls need pictures. And..."

She followed his gaze and sighed, knowing where this was headed. "Christmas trees need ornaments?"

"You know, you're right," he said as though he'd just noticed. "I mean, the tree's magnificent as it is, but a little dressing would improve it."

"It'll need a lot of dressing."

"You're right about that, too!" Ty gave her a delighted smile.

Marlie rolled her eyes and ate more salad. Eventually, he wore her down by not saying anything. "Ty, do you want to go shopping for Christmas ornaments?"

"With you?"

"Yes, with me."

"I wasn't sure." He stood and carried their empty plates to the sink. "You might have been telling me to go by myself."

"Would you?"

He gave her a stern look. "No."

"Just checking. You're going to make me decorate with you, too, right?"

"Yes. I'm going to force holiday merriment on you. Grab your jacket. Santa's Outlet has a 'buy-one-get-one-free' sale going on. *And* I have a ten-percent coupon they gave me when I bought the lights."

He said "coupon." Marlie snickered to herself. Mr. Sophisticated was talking coupons.

However, coupon or not, the outing was going to put a serious ding in her bank balance, Marlie thought as she shrugged into a puffy jacket with a hood.

Ty looked at her incredulously.

"What?"

"Did you bring that with you from Seattle?"

"Yes, why?" She looked down at herself. "What's wrong with it?"

"Nothing, if you're in Seattle. But it's too hot for here." He unzipped her parka and her skin reacted as though she wore nothing beneath it.

"You should ditch the hoodie." Ty met her gaze and slowly pushed the jacket off her shoulders.

Marlie's mouth went dry. Why did it feel as though he was undressing her?

She whipped off her hoodie, feeling exposed even though Ty had seen her in a tank top many times.

He held her parka and she turned her back to slip her arms in the sleeves. Ty brought it up over her shoulders and rested his hands there.

Marlie felt the weight and warmth of his hands through the puffy quilting and was acutely aware of the solid wall of his chest behind her.

Ty's thumbs kneaded the muscles at the base of her neck and traveled outward toward her arms. "You work too hard."

Marlie clamped her eyes shut. She wanted to lean her head against him and let her muscles melt beneath his touch. But she didn't. "I do what I have to."

His hands fell away and Marlie reached for her purse.

"Hey," he said.

Marlie risked a glance upward and met Ty's troubled blue gaze. "If you don't have time for this now, I'll get ornaments."

Go with him, go with him, her heart urged.

Do not bond with him over Christmas ornaments, her mind cautioned.

Live for the moment, live for the moment, said her heart.

"I've got time," she said. *No, you don't!* "I need a break and it'll be fun."

Ty beamed down at her as though she'd granted his fondest wish. It made her a little breathless, him looking at her like that. But while her mind tried to figure out the implications, her heart bounced around happily.

Bounce now, pay later, her mind warned.

Shut up and send me the bill, said her heart.

"You're supposed to have a theme," Ty complained as they unloaded ornaments from the car. "We don't have a theme."

"Yes, we do," Marlie countered with a laugh. "Our theme is Christmas."

Giggling she ran up the stairs. She was carrying big plastic bags of super-sized, light-weight ball ornaments. Ty followed more slowly with the heavier stuff. "We look like we've gorged ourselves at an all-you-can-decorate Christmas buffet."

He'd forgotten about Marlie's inability to decide when presented with too many choices. When she was little, she'd taken forever at the ice cream shop, conning the counter clerks into giving her sample after sample. And hadn't she told him about looking at hundreds of drawer pulls? It's a wonder her house ever got built.

Taking her to a Christmas discount warehouse wasn't the most brilliant idea he'd ever had, except she'd become giddy with excitement, something he hadn't seen in her for years.

To be honest, he was so glad to see that enthusiasm back, he'd have taken her to ten warehouses, if she'd wanted.

Marlie dropped her bags and raced downstairs for another load.

He couldn't believe how much fun they'd had. Marlie had warned him that she had to go back to work when they got home, but Ty's plan was to talk her into decorating the tree now, especially when she was in such a happy, silly mood. It was contagious and Ty felt happier and lighter than he had in a long time. It was so easy being with Marlie—except for the desire that constantly simmered in his veins.

Groundwork first. Tonight, they'd decorate the tree. Another night, he'd seduce her beneath it. He'd feed her food and wine and music and they'd sit and talk by the light of the tree. He'd kiss her until they were both dizzy with wanting. He'd pull back and—this was the important part—tell her he loved her and planned to stick around. Using better words than "stick around," but with that sentiment. Because he'd stuck to his plan of walking the walk before talking the talk, she'd believe him. And then there would be bliss.

Ty was sorting the ornaments when Marlie carried up the last of the bags.

"Why do you have everything in little piles around the tree?" she asked.

"I'm arranging the ornaments by size and type so they'll be distributed evenly within the quadrants."

"Quadrants?" Marlie grinned.

"Front, back, side, side?" Normally, he'd sort by color, as well, but there were so many colors, it wouldn't matter.

She watched him a moment. "What would happen if I just started hanging ornaments on the tree any old way?"

Ty swiveled on one knee to look at her. "Why would you do that?"

"For fun!" She ripped the plastic on a package of oversized

balls, removed one and forced the end of a branch through the wire circle at the top. The red ball stuck out like a clown's nose.

Ty gave her an exasperated look as he stood and pulled it off.

"Ohhh," she said, drawing out the word. "You're one of *those*."

"Those?"

"'Everything-has-to-be-perfect' tree decorators."

He looked down at the piles of ornaments around his feet. Marlie had danced up and down the aisles grabbing everything from angels to snowmen to cartoon characters—and cartoon characters *as* angels. "Not happening here."

Marlie snatched the ball out of his hands.

"Marlie, you need ornament hooks."

Ignoring him, she pushed a branch through the end. "I like the ball sticking out like this."

It looked horrible, but he wasn't going to argue with her about it. Shaking his head, he stepped over the piles to a bulky sack. "Catch." He tossed her a sleeping-bag-sized package of white batting.

"I didn't think you were serious when you said we needed padding under the tree skirt."

Ty ripped the thin plastic on a second bag. "Absolutely." He knelt and began arranging the mounds of white.

Marlie tore into her bag. "Why are we doing this now?"

"You're supposed to put the tree skirt on first."

"There's an order?" She rolled her eyes.

"Skirt, lights, ornaments, garland, and topper."

"What about tinsel?"

He shuddered. "We do not have tinsel." Ty held out his hands for her bag of batting.

She looked like she wanted to drop it on his head instead

of handing it to him. "But if we did, when would we put it on?"

"We will never have tinsel." He compromised on the colored lights. He compromised on the lack of theme. Ty glared at the red bulb on the end of a branch. He even compromised on *ornament* hooks. He drew the line at tinsel. "Where's the tree skirt?"

"Over here somewhere." Marlie moved toward the bags next to the couch. "What's wrong with tinsel?"

Seriously? "It's tacky."

She hooted. "Did you just say 'tacky'?"

"Yes. Tinsel is tacky and it gets everywhere." Ty sat back on his heels and studied the padding he'd carefully mounded to best display the skirt. "It slithers off the branches."

"But it's shiny and glittery and happy." Marlie twirled around with her arms out. "When you walk by, it waves to you."

She made him smile. Clearly, they had Christmas tree compatibility issues. But he didn't care. Except about the tinsel. His parents used it for a time and it would catch on his clothes, especially when he snuck around and tried to figure out what the presents were. Then he'd show up at school with some in his hair and his friends would make fun of him. "Tinsel is lazy decorating," he said. "People stick up an artificial tree and throw tinsel at it and think they're done."

"Maybe they are," Marlie said. "Maybe they don't want nutcrackers, and Santa Clauses, and rocket ships, and wizards and Scooby Doo wearing an elf hat on their tree. Maybe they just want lights and shiny icicles."

Ty leveled a look at her as she searched for the tree skirt in the many, many shopping bags. "Then maybe they shouldn't have gone crazy at the Christmas outlet warehouse."

"Says the person who went crazy at the Christmas tree lot."

Suddenly, Marlie straightened, her back to him, and turned out the room lights.

"Hey, why did—"

Laughing, she spun around, launching the contents of a jumbo bag of tinsel into the air. Glittery clouds of silver floated down, some landing on the tree, some clumping to the floor, but most falling in a shimmery stream all over Ty and Marlie. Mostly Ty.

He got to his feet. "Wha—! You—"

Marlie giggled.

Ty raked his fingers through his hair, staring with loathing at the shiny strands he pulled out. "Tinsel! When did you buy this?"

"While you were bringing the car around. They had bins of it by the checkout stands!"

Yes. He'd seen those bins. He looked from a gleeful Marlie to his defaced tree. From far above his head, tinsel on the highest branches waved at him. A clump slid off the bookshelves behind him and landed on his shoulder.

Marlie exploded with laughter. "You look like Disco Bigfoot!" Marlie was laughing so hard she was bent at the waist, which put her close enough to the floor to grab another handful and rain it down on him.

"Marlie!" He reached for her before she could do it again.

"Oh, Ty, lighten up!" Still laughing, Marlie danced away from him, but her foot slipped on the tinsel-covered wood floor.

Ty clamped his arms around her before she sat down hard. As soon as she had her balance again, she tried to wiggle out of his grasp, but only succeeded in freeing one shoulder. "I'll let you go if you promise to stop with the tinsel."

"Nope!" She pulled at his arms. "Not gonna."

"Marlie, it's nasty stuff. You'll still be finding it next July."

"So I'll clean it up along with the bajillion pine needles I'll find then, too." She struggled forward, slipped, and ended up planting her bottom directly against his crotch.

It was a great fit, to which his body instantly reacted, every nerve coming to attention and letting him know how very much they liked it. He froze, willing her not to move. But Marlie being Marlie, she moved. A lot. His brain told him to let her go, but the rest of him said, "Not quite yet."

Marlie's laughter faded. "Oh." She stilled.

Ty closed his eyes. *Let her go. Let her go while you can.*

Marlie wiggled her hips experimentally, spreading heat and longing through him. "That's either for me or for the tinsel."

Ty bent his head to her hair and inhaled. It smelled like Marlie again. "Not the tinsel," he breathed just above her ear.

Let her go or your plan is a bust.

He squeezed her tighter, so very glad she was back in his arms. In a minute. He'd release her in a minute.

"Mmm." Marlie leaned her head back against his shoulder and slowly rotated her hips against him, pretty much drowning his brain in lust. "Are you going to let me go?"

"I don't want to." Ever.

"I can tell." She moved a little faster, a little harder. "Mmm."

Ty had trouble remembering to breathe. *Inhale. Exhale. Repeat.* Why was remembering to breathe so difficult? He'd been doing it all his life. "Cut it out, Marlie," he said as blood pooled in his groin.

"Why?"

"It's not a good idea." He remembered that, if not the specifics.

"Liar." She tilted her face up. "You think it's a very good idea." And she bit his earlobe, distracting him, and broke free.

"Ha!" She scooped up a clump of tinsel and flung it at the tree.

"Marlie, stop."

She flung faster, her cheeks flushed. "It's either me or the tinsel."

As she reached for more, Ty grabbed her arm and spun her into his chest, face to face. Upon impact, three strips of silver slithered from his head and disappeared down the neckline of her tank top.

"I guess it's me," she said softly.

It's always been you, he thought over the rushing in his ears. And he would tell her when the time was right. The time was not now, in spite of her parted lips and pink cheeks and the wild blond hair that looked as though she'd just got out of bed.

Her chin tilted up and her eyes drifted closed and Ty decided he could use a reminder of why he was laying groundwork. Anyway, he thought as his lips settled against hers, kisses counted as groundwork.

Unless they caused earthquakes the way this one did. Passion, desire, tenderness, and a love that left him completely vulnerable all exploded within him. Zero to sixty in under a second.

Ty inhaled sharply and wrenched his mouth from hers. "I'm not ready for this," he said when he got his breath back.

She rocked her pelvis against him. "Yes, you are."

"No. I mean—I want—" He couldn't even form a complete sentence and he had to tell her that he liked life with her, her kind of life, and he wanted that kind of life now, too. But it was so, so important that Marlie believe him. He loved her. He wouldn't want that life with anyone else—but that didn't mean he only liked it because that's what she wanted, only it did, because he loved her. It was too complicated to explain now.

He dropped his hands and stepped back. "I don't want to mess this up. You're very special to me, Marlie."

HE HAD TO BE KIDDING. Ty did not just give the "you're-very-special" speech to her. He was going to pay.

"Ty!" She gave a good imitation of a laugh. "We're just playing a game. There's nothing to mess up."

"A game?"

"Yeah. The tinsel game." She stepped forward and pulled a piece from his hair over his ear and across his jaw where it snagged on the beginnings of stubble and slipped from her fingers.

Ty swatted at it, sending it onto Marlie's chest to trickle down and join the rest of the tinsel in her bra.

His eyes, dark and hot, stared down at her neckline. His breathing deepened. Marlie's chest rose and fell in time with his.

"Does the tinsel game have rules?" he finally asked.

"When it's no longer fun, you stop playing."

He looked into her eyes for even longer than he'd looked down her top. "How do you play?" he asked and she knew she had him.

"Find the tinsel. Your turn."

Ty lightly drew his fingers over her shoulders and throat. His touch was no heavier than the strips of tinsel, but it was warm where they were cool.

His gaze followed his fingers to her neckline. She felt a tickle and looked down to see that Ty was pulling on one of the strands that had fallen down her shirt.

"That tickles," she told him.

He half-smiled. "Good tickles or bad tickles?"

"They could be better."

He pulled faster and she inhaled in pleased surprise as the tinsel slipped over her skin.

"Better?"

"Yes." Who knew?

"There's more."

She looked down and saw that the first piece he'd withdrawn had brought up a tangle of the other two.

Ty picked up the twisted ends and moved the strands from side to side before pulling them out.

Marlie's breath hitched as gooseflesh raised on her skin. It hadn't been his turn, but she wasn't arguing.

"You've got tinsel all over you," she whispered, and brushed at his hair, an ear, and pulled at the collar of his shirt. "A lot got caught in your collar."

"I feel it."

She tilted her head as though thinking. "The fastest way to get it out would be for you to take off your shirt."

"Wouldn't that be cheating?"

"Wouldn't that be fun?" she countered.

Staring into her eyes, Ty started unbuttoning his shirt.

This was a dangerous game Marlie was playing, this tease and be teased. Ty had been very clear, maybe even insultingly clear, that while he was attracted to her, she shouldn't expect a relationship with him. So Marlie knew that whatever happened between them tonight would be just for tonight. She couldn't say he hadn't warned her and she couldn't say exactly what would happen.

She watched his fingers move from button to button, revealing glints of silver stuck to his skin as the shirt parted. After undoing the last button, he pulled off the shirt in a shower of silver.

Marlie watched his chest rise and fall. Reaching out, she plucked at the silver bits tangled in the light dusting of hair and wanted to wind her arms around him and kiss him until she forgot that he only wanted her for the moment, but not in his life. His chest no longer glittered, but Marlie kept spreading her hands over his skin.

"The game isn't fun anymore," he said and she looked at him, stricken.

He captured her hands and placed them on his heart. She stared at them, feeling his pulse beneath her fingers. "Because, for me, it isn't a game. The first time we kissed, I told you it meant nothing. I was wrong," he admitted. "It meant everything."

Her gaze shot to his face. Ty gave her a crooked smile. "Sorry I short-circuited for a little bit there." He drew a breath. Beneath her palms, his heart picked up speed. "But I'm thinking clearly now. I love you, Marlie."

It was exactly what she wanted to hear and, looking into his eyes, she knew that at this moment, he believed what he was saying. The moment wouldn't last, but she'd take it because it might be the only one she'd ever have.

So she gazed into his dark blue eyes and said, "I loved you even before I was aware of it." He looked at her with such blazing happiness that she knew he would break her heart into so many pieces she'd never put it back together.

"There's more I need to say, but later," he told her.

Marlie wasn't going to think about later.

He kissed her hands before lacing their fingers together. "How do you feel about making love under the Christmas tree?"

She grinned. "You mean, you want me to unwrap your package?"

"Yes." He grinned back. "And I don't want to wait until Christmas."

"Oh, we're not." She reached for his belt, but Ty swooped

down and captured her mouth with his, swallowing her startled squeak, trapping her hands between their bodies.

Heat washed over her. Ty kissed her full on as though this was a continuation of the kiss that started it all. Marlie instantly lost herself in the kiss. This was how it was between them—all or nothing. No in between. No gentle warm up. Just everything at once.

Ty's hands were flat against her back, one dipping to her waist to skim beneath her thin cotton tank.

He pressed her back until her feet no longer held her and he did, kneeling and lowering her to the floor. He straightened and she smiled to see his head surrounded by colored lights. He undid all his careful mounds of batting and smoothed them into a cushion, picking off bits of silver. "I do hate tinsel," he said without heat.

"I can make you like it."

"Not possible."

"Close your eyes."

He did and Marlie sat up and whipped off her tank top. It was no big deal because she wore a wide sports bra beneath. But this is where it got interesting. There was no graceful way to get out of the thing, so she really hoped he wasn't peeking.

"I'm turning around," he said, solving her problem. "I want to get into the cabinet."

"Why?"

"I told you I had plans. Only I planned for the tree to be decorated before I carried them out."

"It is decorated," she protested, wiggling out of the stretchy sports bra.

"Someday, I'll show you decorated."

"You'll come around." She covered her torso in tinsel and leaned back on her elbows. "Ready."

Ty set a small wooden box off to the side and turned to

look at her. He froze on all fours. For long moments he stared, and Marlie tracked his gaze by the movements of his eyes. "Wow." Smiling slightly, he crawled over to her. "You make a very persuasive argument, but the tinsel is still in the way." As he lowered himself onto his stomach, he exhaled. The puff of air caused a tiny silver avalanche. The movement caught his attention. "I'm seeing possibilities here."

Marlie felt more tinsel slide with every breath she took, so she was trying not to breathe very much.

Ty blew a gentle stream of air that made Marlie's stomach contract. Tinsel flowed into the hollow.

His gaze heated and became very focused. Marlie looked down at herself and saw her nipples poking through the silver, revealing themselves a little quicker than she'd anticipated. Too bad. She'd just have to brazen it out.

Ty blew another stream and tinsel slithered over her ribcage. Marlie gulped air, which sent more tinsel rolling sideways, tickling her skin.

"I am officially a fan," Ty announced. "You can wear all the tinsel you want."

"What about the tree?"

"I don't want to kiss the tree." He leaned over her. "And I don't want the tree to kiss me."

"But—" His hand covered her breast right then and she forgot what she'd been going to argue. Or why. She'd been thinking about his touch, wanting it again. So now plain old relief overwhelmed everything else. And then plain old relief gave way to old-fashioned lust. "Ty," she breathed right before he kissed her.

Marlie's quivering arms collapsed. The soft batting surrounded her as Ty kissed her with long, deep, drugging kisses that made her dizzy with wanting.

She ran her hands over his back and drew her foot up his denim-clad leg. Ty dragged his mouth from hers. "I forgot to tell you you're beautiful. I meant to tell you. You're so beautiful. So beautiful."

Great sentiment. Limited vocabulary.

"Incredibly beautiful."

"And hot," Marlie said.

"Yes. Hot. So hot. Incredi—"

"I mean, sweaty hot." She raised an arm to show him the tinsel stuck to it.

Ty blinked passion-glazed eyes. She'd done that. She had turned her handsome hunk of a roommate into a babbling love zombie.

He sucked in air. "You're hot."

"Yeah."

"This kind of hot." He reached for the snap on her jeans.

"Shoes and socks first," she said.

He grinned. "You mean there's an order?"

"Shoes, socks, jeans, underwear. Which is logical, unlike your tree-decorating rules." Marlie unzipped her boots and let Ty pull them off.

"You're so beautiful," he repeated, going a bit glassy-eyed again and losing track of what they were doing.

"So are you. Take off your jeans."

They struggled to undress without getting out from beneath the tree.

Naked, Ty looked down at himself. "When do we take off the tinsel?"

"Tinsel chooses you—you don't choose the tinsel," Marlie told him. Then she hung tinsel where no tinsel had ever hung before.

"My manhood is suffering," Ty complained.

"Your manhood is all silver and sparkly," Marlie said admiringly.

"Exactly what every guy wants to hear." As he spoke, Ty collected strands and made a brush. "Your turn."

Propping himself on an elbow, he dragged the ends over Marlie's stomach, tickling her and continued over her breasts and neck, down her arms and thighs. The tickles turned teasing and then maddening as she craved a firmer touch. "Ty! Enough!"

"I thought you liked tinsel."

Marlie blinked some of the lust from her eyes to see his clear ones gazing back at her. She should do something about that. "I like a lot of things." She gave him a small smile and let her legs fall open as she drew her fingers down her stomach and pressed them between her thighs.

His eyes went slightly unfocused. Marlie threw in a moan.

"Let me help you with that." He rolled on top of her, his fingers replacing hers.

Much better. Her next moan was real and ended on a gasp as Ty's mouth closed over her breast. Muuuuch better.

They kissed and touched and explored each other and the heat that had been simmering between them for days, maybe years, erupted until Marlie couldn't stand it. "Ty," she groaned. "I need you inside me." She'd wanted before, but she'd never *needed*.

He moved back and she reached for him, but he was rolling on a condom. The wooden box was open.

"Why do you keep condoms in the living room? Don't answer that."

"I had plans, remember?" He leaned over her. "I love you, Marlie."

He gazed at her, all heart-breakingly sincere and Marlie chose to focus on the sincere part and deal with the heart breaking later.

She pulled him to her. "Can you love me a little faster?"

He smiled against her mouth until she bit him on the lip so he'd realize she meant business. Seconds later, he pushed inside, slow and steady, filling her and becoming her friend *and* lover.

This is why he'll break your heart, she thought. *It'll never be like this with anyone else.* She buried her nose in the spot where his neck met his shoulder and sighed.

He stilled. "You okay?"

"Well, not *now*."

"Oh—"

"No, dummy. Because you stopped."

He drew back so he could see her. "But you sighed and it wasn't a good sigh."

He'd heard that? "I was thinking that I'd known you since before you had a great chest."

A grin split his face. "What a coincidence. I was thinking the same thing."

She felt herself grin back. *This is my moment. This is the one I'm keeping. This one, when we're joined together and he's looking at me with love and he hasn't broken my heart yet.*

Ty dipped his head and Marlie knew he meant to kiss her gently, but as always, the heat flared, bringing her to an instant boil.

Groaning, he started moving again. "How did we miss this, Marlie?"

"Maybe we weren't ready to handle it until now."

"I'm so ready," he exhaled next to her ear. "Tell me you're ready."

Marlie closed her eyes, drawing out the moment, deliberately imprinting the weight of him, the quiver in his arms as he held his full weight off her, the heat of their bodies, the sound of their breathing and the more intimate sound of moist flesh rubbing against moist flesh. She inhaled his scent, knowing it would be forever mixed with pine in her memories. She wanted to remember the way he filled her, the catch in his voice as he murmured her name, the softness of his hair.

And most especially, she wanted to remember one, piercingly sweet moment of pleasure. She licked his earlobe, tasting him, and then nipped it with her lips. "Ready."

As he rocked against her, Marlie wrapped her legs around him and held on while the tension built faster and tighter than ever before. She'd wanted her moment of pleasure, but she got an explosion of moments. Marlie actually saw colored stars as pleasure rippled through her. The stars were still there as Ty shuddered his own release and while he breathed her name as he kissed each eyelid.

When she opened her eyes, she saw that the stars were the Christmas tree lights above her, reflected in tinsel and in Ty's shining eyes.

"Wow. So that's the way sex is supposed to be." He knuckled a strand of damp hair off her cheek.

"Good to know," she said lightly.

Ty rolled to her side and drew her head to his shoulder. They lay on their backs, looking up through the tree branches.

"Do you think it'll always be like that?" he asked. "Or was that a one-time lust bomb?"

Lust bomb was actually a good description. "Depends on who you're having sex with, I suppose."

He turned his head. "With you!" he said, sounding outraged.

And right then, Marlie decided she wanted another moment. "Is the wooden box empty?"

"It will never be empty, and there will be wooden boxes in every room in the house," Ty vowed.

"Then let's find out," Marlie said, and reached for him.

14

MARLIE WAS FLOATING. Floating.

That's what the best sex of your life will do to you. Tra la la. She hummed. Her body hummed. She loved Ty and Ty loved her and the world was a wonderful place, a wonderful glittery, silvery place.

Maybe she'd take him with her to the Highland games this weekend. She still wanted to see the drummer compete in the pipe and drum competition. Alicia, the reporter, needed an ending to her series and did Marlie ever have an ending for her. After last night, she actually dared to believe that her moment with Ty might not have to end.

She couldn't stop smiling as she turned on her computer. Even though she'd have to work like a mad woman to be able to take the weekend off, Marlie grinned until her cheeks were sore.

Sex was clearly good for the brain because she was on fire with brilliance. She'd hoped that Ty would come home during lunch because she wanted a nooner. Marlie had never had a nooner because Eric's office had been too far away from their apartment. Today was doubtful because she'd had a morninger and Ty had been late to work.

She sighed happily. There was always tonight.

Marlie worked until she heard a distant jazzy tune. Following the sound upstairs, she realized it was Ty's cell phone. He must have forgotten it this morning. She laughed. He'd been distracted.

Wow, there were a lot of missed calls. What an excellent excuse to phone his office.

"I wonder if you could help me," she said when he answered. "I seem to be missing some tinsel."

He chuckled. "It's in my shoes. And car."

"And pants?"

"I don't know." He lowered his voice. "You can check when I get home."

"I will check *very* carefully, in *all* your nooks and crannies."

"I can think of places where we can look for it, too."

Marlie could hear office sounds around him and figured he couldn't get too explicit. "Hey, listen, not that this isn't fun, but I actually called because you left your cell phone here this morning."

"Yeah, I noticed that."

"You've got nine missed calls."

"That many? Who are they from?"

Spoken like a man with nothing to hide. Smiling, Marlie opened the list. "Seven are from your builder." Probably in connection with Ty backing out of buying the townhouse. They hadn't discussed it, but there was certainly no reason for him to buy it now. He already said he liked hers better anyway. How convenient that all he had to do was move down the hall.

Ty exhaled. "I'm supposed to choose fixtures and countertops. He wants to order before the end of the year. I've been waiting for months, and now he wants instant decisions. I already chose everything once, but it was so long ago, some of the things have been discontinued. So now I have to start over."

That wasn't what Marlie expected to hear.

"I know you remember what it was like making about a thousand little decisions when you bought your place."

"I remember."

Ty laughed, apparently oblivious to her strained voice. "I'm not going to be nearly so picky."

"Maybe you can visit the showroom after work." *Invite me along. At least invite me along.*

He lowered his voice. "I have plans with you after work."

Plans that obviously didn't include her in anything long term.

She couldn't. She just couldn't. He was still going through with the purchase of his house. He was picking *fixtures* for his house. By himself. He hadn't asked for her input and the only reason why was because she wouldn't be living there with him.

Their moment was over. He loved her, but he was still going on with the kind of life he'd planned for himself. Well, Marlie was not going to be his bed buddy for the next six weeks or however long it would be until he moved out. "I—I actually have a chance to earn a couple thousand extra dollars if I can do a quick turnaround on a site redesign," she told him. "I've been slacking off lately and if I put in the time, I can avoid dipping into my savings for the mortgage payment."

He was supposed to say, "But you don't have to worry about the mortgage payment because I won't be moving out."

But what he said was, "Okay." It was a disappointed "okay," but it wasn't what Marlie needed to hear.

"Maybe I will stop by the showroom then," he added, making it worse. He did have a way of making things worse.

MAYBE SHE WAS TIRED, Ty thought as he disconnected the phone.

Tired enough to fall asleep on her office loveseat, he saw later. He'd been thinking about her all day and how being with her was phenomenally better than he'd ever dreamed. But they hadn't got much sleep last night. He looked down at her, feeling his chest grow tight with emotion. She was the one for him. It was so clear now, he marveled that he'd had no inkling of it before.

He pulled the throw over her shoulder, which he'd done lots of times in the past, and placed a light kiss on her temple, which he had not.

She didn't stir, so he quietly left. There was always tomorrow morning and the entire weekend to look forward to. In the meantime, Ty cleaned up the tinsel, leaving a few strays on the tree, and tossed or packed up the empty ornament boxes left over from their middle-of-the-night naked tree decorating, something he planned to make an annual tradition.

Marlie was gone when he woke up the next morning. But, oh, look, she'd left a sexy little note on the fridge. "Gone to Highland games. Back late. Marlie." Not even "love, Marlie."

She'd rather spend Saturday with her piper date than making love with him? She didn't even wake him up to say good-bye? Ty felt as though he'd been punched in the stomach. Or higher—in the heart. Something was wrong and he wasn't going to try to tell himself he was overreacting.

He did not hallucinate the other night. Had he not been clear that he loved her? What was going on in that head of hers?

Ty got dressed because he was not waiting for tonight to ask her.

THE MOURNFUL CRY OF THE bagpipes exactly matched Marlie's mood. Her date thought she was moved to tears by the music and bought her a CD of bagpipe music put out by a local high school.

How could Ty walk away from what they'd shared? Oh, sure, he wasn't planning to walk away until they'd shared for a few more weeks, but that he already assumed he'd leave just made it worse. She'd known he'd break her heart, but he'd kept telling her he loved her, and so she'd let herself hope.

How could she do that to herself? How could she fall in love with another man who didn't want to build a life with her?

After several hours of faking it, Marlie was actually beginning to enjoy herself as she and her date attempted Scottish Country Dancing.

Laughing afterward, she waited beneath an awning set up over picnic tables as her date got them something to drink.

The instant he turned his back to walk away, the *very* instant, someone sat across the table from her. Ty.

"What the hell, Marlie?" was his opener.

"Back 'atcha."

"You're avoiding me," he said.

Marlie supposed a crowd was as good a place as any to have this discussion. "Not on purpose," she lied. "But taking a couple of days to cool off is a good idea. The other night was pretty intense and neither of us wants to rush into anything."

His expression hardened. "We've known each other all our lives. That's not rushing."

"That doesn't mean we want the same things."

"We don't have to. You get your way sometimes, I get my way sometimes, and other times, we compromise."

"You shouldn't compromise on the big stuff," Marlie said at the same time Ty's jazzy ringtone sounded.

He reached for his cell.

He's answering his phone while we're having a serious life discussion.

"I've been trying to..." He checked to see who was calling. "I've got to talk to her." He held the phone to his ear. "Axelle?"

Axelle? Discussion over. So over.

Marlie pushed herself up and with shaky legs, climbed over the wooden bench. She saw her date headed her way, and with him was Alicia and her cameraman. Marlie had never been so glad to see the reporter.

By the time she finished the interview, Ty was gone and Marlie had a pretty good idea where.

TY WAITED UP FOR MARLIE beneath the Christmas tree.

"What did I do wrong?" he asked when she sat on the floor beside him. "Because I know it was something."

"Ty..."

"Is it because I had to leave? I tried to get your attention to tell you, but you were being interviewed."

She turned her blank Marlie gaze on him, the one he never thought he'd see again. This wasn't good.

"I think we're better as friends," Marlie told him, apparently serious.

"I don't," Ty said. "And you don't either. Want me to remind you why?"

She glared at him. "Were you going to ask me to move into your house?"

"No." He was surprised. "Why would I do that?"

"Well, then." She got to her feet.

So did he. "Marlie, do you *want* to live in my house?"

"No." She shook her head. "I like my house."

"I like your house, too." He drew her close. "But I love you. I want to be with you."

Her mouth twisted. "For how long?"

"What kind of question is that?" Ty pulled back to search her face.

"A realistic one. You've bounced around from place to place and from girlfriend to girlfriend."

"Not anymore, I won't."

"You say that now, but you have very specific ideas about your life," she said.

"So do you! Anyway, I like yours now," he reminded her. He'd mentioned that before, hadn't he?

"Since when?"

Maybe not. "Since I fell in love with you."

"And yet, you're buying a house so you can move out."

Was that what was bothering her? "I have a contract, Marlie. I have to buy it."

"You didn't even ask me to pick the fixtures!"

She wanted to break up over hardware? "You're not going to live there! Anyway, you would have taken forever to choose."

She gave him a wounded look.

"Marlie." He chuckled and folded her into his arms. "I like that you're careful making decisions and I appreciate you wanting to help. But don't worry about it. Axelle's going to choose them. It's all taken care of."

Marlie stiffened immediately and if Ty hadn't been distracted by how good it felt to hold her close again, he'd have anticipated how that would sound to her.

She pushed out of his arms. "Yes, I noticed how you couldn't wait to take her call while talking with me!"

Yeah, that probably didn't look too great, either. "I'm sorry, but I'd been trying reach her. I've got this time crunch with the builder and things have been so crazy at work, I never made it to the showroom."

"Oh." She backed up, arms across her torso. "Well, let

me save you some time. Don't bother coming to the games tomorrow. That should free up your day."

"I can't go anyway," he told her. "I've got to go into work."

"On *Sunday?*"

"The company is reorganizing and trying to get stuff nailed down before the end of the year. I might have to start traveling again."

"Then I guess I'll see you around." She turned to leave.

"See me around?" He took a step toward her and stopped when she backed up again. "What's wrong? This can't be about Axelle choosing stuff for the house."

She wouldn't meet his eyes.

"It *is?*"

"Not *just* that."

Ty had an ugly thought. "Marlie, tell me you're not mad because you think there's something going on between me and Axelle."

She shot him a look. "Is there?"

Ty stared at her, unbelievably stung by the question. "You think I'm the kind of man who—" He broke off, unwilling to finish.

"No," Marlie admitted, and he exhaled. "But I do think you live in the moment and I think our moment is over. Or it will be once you start traveling and someone else catches your interest."

"That's insulting."

She shook her head. "I don't mean it to be. I'm being realistic and so should you."

"You're kidding."

But she wasn't.

And that's why he should have stuck to the plan, Ty thought as Marlie went upstairs. She was afraid he'd grow bored and leave. The irony was that he was going in on a Sunday to try to avoid the travel. He could talk all night long, but she wouldn't believe him. He'd failed to lay the proper groundwork and now he'd have to find another way to convince her that she was going to be stuck with him for the rest of her life.

WHEN MARLIE GOT HOME from her twelfth date, she found Ty sitting on the couch and watching TV while eating junk food.

It was as though they'd never slept together, as if she'd never learned his body or lost her mind with pleasure.

He tilted a bottle of water and she admired his manly neck as he drank. Yes, everything was back the way it had been. Except Marlie. She'd never be the same again.

She sat on the couch next to Ty and he held out his hand. She dropped yesterday's piper charm and the drum charm from today into his palm, hesitated, and unfastened her bracelet.

Best not tempt fate by getting too close.

"How was the competition?" Ty asked.

"Loud," Marlie said. "How was work?"

"Work was great. Especially after I quit."

"What?"

He squinted at her bracelet as he worked the pliers. "I quit."

"Your job?"

"Yes."

Marlie stared at him. "Why?"

He glanced at her and then back at the bracelet. "They wanted to transfer me to Azerbaijan."

"Oh."

"I said no. They thought I was holding out for more money." He finished attaching one charm and started on another. "But I told them I was holding out for you, and you're living in your dream house, and I wanted to live in it with you."

"You quit your job for me?"

"Well, for us. And the house." He stopped working to look at her. "Are you impressed?"

"Impressed isn't the right word." Horrified was the right word. Ty didn't need to hear the right word.

"You don't look impressed," he said.

"You're unemployed. I'm worried about the rent." And another thought occurred to her. "What about your house?"

"Ah. There has been a development on that front, as well."

Marlie braced herself.

"After we discussed Axelle and the fixtures, I realized you were lacking a crucial piece of information." He carefully closed the charm's jump ring. "The reason Axelle is selecting everything is because she's buying the house."

"You sold her your house?" Marlie's jaw dropped.

"Not immediately. She'll rent for a few months until she's confident the restaurant is on its feet." Ty studied her. "Still not impressed, I see."

"Impressed that you're unemployed *and* homeless?"

"I was hoping you'd get past the facts and admire the gestures, but in case you didn't…" He spun his finger in a circle, indicating that she should turn around.

Marlie looked over her shoulder and there was the tree, all seventeen feet of it covered in tinsel. No clumps, all strands hanging straight, except for the ones waving in the air from the vents.

Her heart started thudding. He was serious. He'd quit his job and sold his house, but nothing said "I love you" like a seventeen foot Christmas tree covered in tinsel.

She turned back to him. "I am very impressed," she said. Later, she'd tell him she didn't care about tinsel one way or another and that she'd only bought it to use as stuffing in gift bags for her clients.

"Good." He took her wrist and fastened the bracelet around it. "Although if that hadn't made my point, I figured this would."

"Yes, buying me twelve dates was very impressive," she said. Twelve men and not one of them touched her heart like he did. Marlie moved the bracelet so she could admire all the charms, but noticed that the spacing was crowded near the clasp. She started to say something about it to Ty, and that's when she saw the thirteenth charm. A heart. A heart with engraving on it. She tilted it to the light in order to read the words: *True Love.*

In her mind, she heard the carol...*my true love gave to me...* She caught her breath and looked up to find Ty watching her.

"I love you, Marlie. And I want you to know that you've got my heart and you'll always have it, whether you want it or not."

She squeezed the bracelet. "I want it. I've always wanted it."

Ty kissed her until her own heart beat against its restraints. *Oh, go ahead,* she told it and set it free. *Fall in love with him.*

Marlie kissed him until she was dizzy and breathless, and then dragged in a lungful of air and kissed him some more. "I love that you quit your job, sold your house, and gave me your heart, but the tinsel clinched the deal."

"Is the deal marriage?" he asked, breathing heavily. "Because I want to marry you, Marlie. I want to be everything on your list."

Marlie said, "Since we talked, I've added passion to my list."

"I added that," Ty said. "Want me to add it again?"

"In a minute."

"You're killing me." Ty touched his forehead to hers. "What now?"

"Ty…I can't believe I'm saying this, but however corny, 'home *is* where the heart is', so while I appreciate you quitting your job more than I can say, maybe you can get it back. If I have to sell my house to follow you, then I will." If she had to *give* it away in order to follow him, she would. He would never leave her. He never had.

He lifted his head, his eyes dark with emotion. "You said you'd never do that again."

"I know, I know. But I'd rather be with you than stay in this house."

"But this is your dream house."

"It's not about the house," Marlie told him. "It's about building a life with you."

He smiled. "So that's a 'yes' to the marriage question."

"There was no question."

"Are you going to call your mom and tell her about us?"

Marlie nodded. "As soon as she gets back from the cruise."

"Then we're officially engaged." He exhaled and closed his eyes. "Let me just enjoy this moment."

"It would be more enjoyable if we were kissing," Marlie pointed out.

He held up a finger and then opened his eyes. "You know how you just agreed to sell your house and marry a homeless, heartless, unemployed person?"

"I may be rethinking that."

He grinned. "I'm technically only unemployed until I start work in a different division after Christmas. I'm just changing floors."

She pushed at his shoulder. "You let me believe you quit your job!"

"I did quit. And then I walked upstairs and got another one."

"But still!"

"This is good news, Marlie." He reached for her. "I've got a couple of weeks off. We can scout wedding venues."

"That's a blatant bribe."

"Yes."

"And I'll take that bribe." Marlie leaned into him and unbuttoned his shirt. Putting her palm over his chest, she said, "But right now, you're going to show me where you're planning to keep my heart."

* * * * *

*Harlequin Presents® is thrilled
to introduce the first installment of
an epic tale of passion and drama by*
**USA TODAY Bestselling Author
Penny Jordan***!*

*When buttoned-up Giselle first meets
the devastatingly handsome Saul Parenti,
the heat between them is explosive....*

"LET ME GET THIS STRAIGHT. Are you actually suggesting that I would stoop to that kind of game playing?"

Saul came out from behind his desk and walked toward her. Giselle could smell his hot male scent and it was making her dizzy, igniting a low, dull, pulsing ache that was taking over her whole body.

Giselle defended her suspicions. "You don't want me here."

"No," Saul agreed, "I don't."

And then he did what he had sworn he would not do, cursing himself beneath his breath as he reached for her, pulling her fiercely into his arms and kissing her with all the pent-up fury she had aroused in him from the moment he had first seen her.

Giselle certainly *wanted* to resist him. But the hand she raised to push him away developed a will of its own and was sliding along his bare arm beneath the sleeve of his shirt, and the body that should have been arching away from him was instead melting into him.

Beneath the pressure of his kiss he could feel and taste her gasp of undeniable response to him. He wanted to devour her, take her and drive them both until they were equally satiated—even whilst the anger within him that she should make him feel that way roared and burned its resentment of his need.

She was helpless, Giselle recognized, totally unable to withstand the storm lashing at her, able only to cling to the man who was the cause of it and pray that she would survive.

Somewhere else in the building a door banged. The sound exploded into the sensual tension that had enclosed them, driving them apart. Saul's chest was rising and falling as he fought for control; Giselle's whole body was trembling.

Without a word she turned and ran.

Find out what happens when Saul and Giselle succumb to their irresistible desire in

THE RELUCTANT SURRENDER

Available January 2011 from Harlequin Presents®

HARLEQUIN®

A Romance

FOR EVERY MOOD™

Spotlight on

Classic

Quintessential, modern love stories
that are romance at its finest.

See the next page
to enjoy a sneak peek from
the Harlequin Presents® series.

Silhouette Desire

HAVE BABY,
NEED BILLIONAIRE

MAUREEN CHILD

Simon Bradley is accomplished, successful
and very proud. The fact that he has to
prove he's fit to be a father to his own child
is preposterous. Especially when he has to
prove it to Tula Barrons, one of the most
scatterbrained women he's ever met. But Simon
has a ruthless plan to win Tula over and when
passion overrules prudence one night, it opens
up the door to an affair that leaves them both
staggering. Will this billionaire bachelor learn
to love more than his fortune?

*Billionaires
and Babies*

*Available January
wherever books are sold.*

Always Powerful, Passionate and Provocative.

Visit Silhouette Books at www.eHarlequin.com

SD73072

REQUEST YOUR FREE BOOKS!

HARLEQUIN®

Blaze™

Red-hot reads!

2 FREE NOVELS PLUS 2 FREE GIFTS!

YES! Please send me 2 FREE Harlequin® Blaze™ novels and my 2 FREE gifts (gifts are worth about $10). After receiving them, if I don't wish to receive any more books, I can return the shipping statement marked "cancel." If I don't cancel, I will receive 6 brand-new novels every month and be billed just $4.24 per book in the U.S. or $4.71 per book in Canada. That's a saving of at least 15% off the cover price. It's quite a bargain. Shipping and handling is just 50¢ per book.* I understand that accepting the 2 free books and gifts places me under no obligation to buy anything. I can always return a shipment and cancel at any time. Even if I never buy another book, the two free books and gifts are mine to keep forever.

151/351 HDN E5LS

Name _____ (PLEASE PRINT) _____

Address _____ Apt. # _____

City _____ State/Prov. _____ Zip/Postal Code _____

Signature (if under 18, a parent or guardian must sign) _____

Mail to the **Harlequin Reader Service:**
IN U.S.A.: P.O. Box 1867, Buffalo, NY 14240-1867
IN CANADA: P.O. Box 609, Fort Erie, Ontario L2A 5X3

Not valid for current subscribers to Harlequin Blaze books.

Want to try two free books from another line?
Call 1-800-873-8635 or visit www.morefreebooks.com.

* Terms and prices subject to change without notice. Prices do not include applicable taxes. N.Y. residents add applicable sales tax. Canadian residents will be charged applicable provincial taxes and GST. Offer not valid in Quebec. This offer is limited to one order per household. All orders subject to approval. Credit or debit balances in a customer's account(s) may be offset by any other outstanding balance owed by or to the customer. Please allow 4 to 6 weeks for delivery. Offer available while quantities last.

Your Privacy: Harlequin Books is committed to protecting your privacy. Our Privacy Policy is available online at www.eHarlequin.com or upon request from the Reader Service. From time to time we make our lists of customers available to reputable third parties who may have a product or service of interest to you. If you would prefer we not share your name and address, please check here. ☐

Help us get it right—We strive for accurate, respectful and relevant communications. To clarify or modify your communication preferences, visit us at www.ReaderService.com/consumerschoice.

HARLEQUIN *Blaze*

COMING NEXT MONTH

Available December 28, 2010

#585 INTO THE NIGHT
Forbidden Fantasies
Kate Hoffmann

#586 THE REBEL
Uniformly Hot!
Rhonda Nelson

#587 IRRESISTIBLE FORTUNE
Wendy Etherington

#588 CAUGHT OFF GUARD
Kira Sinclair

#589 SEALed WITH A KISS
Jill Monroe

#590 JUMP START
Texas Hotzone
Lisa Renee Jones